For more than forty years,
Yearling has been the leading name
in classic and award-winning literature
for young readers.

Yearling books feature children's
favorite authors and characters,
providing dynamic stories of adventure,
humor, history, mystery, and fantasy.

Trust Yearling paperbacks to entertain,
inspire, and promote the love of reading
in all children.

OTHER YEARLING BOOKS
YOU WILL ENJOY

The CAPED 6TH GRADER

2

Totally Toxic

Zoe Quinn

ILLUSTRATED BY BRIE SPANGLER

A YEARLING BOOK

Visit us on the Web! www.randomhouse.com/kids

Educators and librarians, for a variety of teaching tools, visit us at
www.randomhouse.com/teachers

ISBN-13: 978-0-440-42080-4
ISBN-10: 0-440-42080-6
GLB ISBN-13: 978-0-385-90305-9
GLB ISBN-10: 0-385-90305-7

Printed in the United States of America

June 2006

10 9 8 7 6 5 4 3 2 1

CHAPTER

1

THE superhero training manual was open to page ninety-four. I was sprawled across my puffy pink and green comforter, but in the last hour I'd barely glanced at the book. Instead, I'd been reading my newest Lightning Girl comic book; then I had started sorting through photos and other souvenirs from the school play. I was *supposed* to be studying for the superhero test, but I was entitled to a little "research"—the photos weren't going to put *themselves* into the album, right?

Smiling, I slid a photo of Howie Hunt into one of the pages. It was a great picture of him as Prince Irving St. Ives, snapped during his dance number.

Not that I needed a photograph to remind me. If I live to be five hundred years old (and who knows . . . I just might), I will never forget Howie Hunt's performance—or any other moment of the sixth-grade play. After all, it was not only a great theatrical success, but it also happened to be the most exciting drama production in the history of Sweetbriar Middle School.

Of course, I was the only one who knew that. Me, and my grandpa Zack.

I plucked the program from the pile of flyers and ticket stubs and glanced through it. I was listed as a member of the stage crew. But that wasn't the half of it.

Not to brag or anything, but I, Zoe Richards, single-handedly prevented the production from being a full-on catastrophe. To be more specific, I used my superpowers.

Yep—I've got superpowers. And if you're surprised, think how I felt when I found out! Strange things began to happen to me on my twelfth birthday, the kind of things that don't happen in real life, you know? Like being able to outrun the school bus and lift cars with my bare hands. I was confused, to say the least, since I (like most intelligent, logical kids) figured superpowers were the stuff of comic books and action movies. But my grandpa Zack set me straight:

"Think of these powers as a special kind of talent you never knew you had. Being a superhero is, in the truest sense, part of who you already are: Zoe Richards. Nothing can ever change that."

Grandpa knew what he was talking about, of course. He isn't just the proprietor of Sweetbriar's premier dry-cleaning store; he used to be a superhero, too. Even though he retired several years ago, he had one last task to perform for the Superhero Federation (oh, yes—did I mention that we have our own federation? Kind of like a PTA with extras). Now that he was sure I had inherited the superhero gene, it was his job to steer me through the early phases of my hero-ness, using the superhero training manual as a study guide. (Remember the superhero manual? The one I was supposed to be reading instead of pasting snapshots into my photo album?)

Anyway, during a rehearsal for the school play, I'd used my very new superpowers to stop a giant stage light from crashing down on Howie's head in the middle of his tap-dance routine. Boy, would *that* have messed up his rhythm . . . not to mention the fact that it probably would have killed him!

The good news was that Howie walked away without a scratch, and nobody knew how close we'd come to disaster. The bad news was that as an apprentice hero, I really shouldn't have been using my superpowers at all. If the Superhero Federation were to find out (and I'm pretty sure they have ways of detecting that sort of stuff), I could be in for a major reprimand. Or worse. Looking at the photos of Howie reminded me of just how much trouble I could be in, right that very minute. . . .

My worrying was interrupted by the sound of footsteps in the hall. Reaching over the stacks of photos, I grabbed the superhero manual and tucked it under my comforter just as my mother came through my bedroom door. She was carrying a laundry basket filled with folded clothes. She was frowning down at the clean laundry like she had no idea what to do with it.

"Hi, Mom."

My voice startled her out of her daze, and she looked up from the basket. From across the room I caught a whiff of the flower-scented, just-washed clothes.

"Oh, hi, kiddo. Here's your laundry." She placed the basket on the foot of my bed and smoothed a wrinkle from a sweatshirt that lay on top of the pile. "Nice and clean and still warm from the dryer."

I squinted at her. "You okay?"

"Hmmm? Oh, I'm fine. Just thinking about something."

"Something" could only mean one thing: a Big Thing. Mom doesn't waste time worrying about the small stuff in her life. If she was mulling something over, it had to involve the environment, or social injustice, or animal rights, or some other issue that needed a major campaign.

I sat up on the bed and moved some of the snapshots so I could scoot toward the basket. "Did you wash my gray T-shirt with the yellow sleeves?"

"I think so. It's probably at the bottom of the pile. . . ."

"Great!" I snatched the sweatshirt out of the basket and dropped it on the bed. "'Cause I want to wear it tomorrow." I began digging in the snuggly-warm pile for the T-shirt.

"Zoe!"

"Did you wash the camouflage cargo pants?" I grabbed a handful of socks from the basket and dropped them on the bed. "You know, the ones with the broken zipper on the side pocket? Emily says they go great with the T-shirt."

"Zoe, I just folded those!" Mom shook her head and bent down to pick up the socks.

"Don't worry," I told her, smiling as I tossed aside a pair of flannel pajama pants and leaned into the basket. "I'll put everything away as soon as I—"

WHOA!

I fell backward onto the pillows as if I'd been shoved. The room seemed to spin, and my eyes burned. I sucked in a deep breath, but that only made me dizzier.

4

Since I'd never experienced anything like that before, I couldn't help wondering if the reaction was superpower related. That would certainly explain why Mom wasn't gasping for breath like me. Luckily, she was on her knees at the foot of the bed, reaching underneath it to retrieve a yellow argyle, and didn't notice that I was clutching the headboard for dear life.

It was the scent! It was everywhere, like an explosion from the depths of the laundry basket, like some crazy chemistry experiment gone bad . . . only it smelled *good*. Really good, like . . . like . . .

Well, like mountain springwater.

Or fresh country air. Ocean breeze, summer rain . . .

The aroma drifted up to choke me as familiar phrases from fabric softener and detergent commercials rang in my head. . . .

Sunshine bouquet, wildflower soft, autumn sunrise . . .

And even though the smell was pleasant, it was so intense I was sure I was going to hurl!

I gave the laundry basket a good hard kick, toppling it off the bed. The clothes tumbled onto the floor, taking their aroma with them. I could still smell the waterfall-fresh fragrance, but it was farther away, less overpowering. The spinning slowed and I could breathe again.

Mom stood up, clutching the socks. Her eyes went from the overturned basket to the pile of crumpled clothes on the floor.

I gave her a weak smile, hoping she wouldn't notice that my eyes were still a little watery. "It was an accident," I said, my voice raspy. "Sorry."

For a minute, I thought she was going to yell at me and tell me to pick up every piece of clothing. But she didn't. Instead, she sat down on the bed, absently tossing T-shirts and underwear back into the basket, staring vaguely at the Lightning Girl poster above the headboard.

Boy! She really was lost in thought. Whatever activist issue she was thinking about must have been a biggie. Like, on a global scale.

"What's wrong?" I asked.

"Oh, I was just thinking about that new factory that opened outside town."

I pictured the sprawling cement building with its three tall smokestacks, and the high chain-link fence surrounding the property. A massive full-color board outside announced that it was the property of Mitchell Enterprises. "What about it?"

"They manufacture household soap products. The detergent I used on this load of laundry is one of their new brands."

Hmmm, interesting. Maybe my dizziness had something to do with the detergent. What the heck was in this stuff that nearly knocked me out?

"I'm not going to use it anymore, though." Mom let out a long sigh. "I've heard some terrible rumors."

"WHAT RUMORS?"

"I'm not sure this factory is . . . well . . . on the up-and-up."

On the up-and-up. It was one of those expressions grown-ups used when they didn't want to scare you. I frowned knowingly.

"You mean, the factory is an evil presence, poised to wreak havoc on our innocent village?" (*That* was one of the expressions Lightning Girl's commander used when he was about to dispatch her on a major, gnarly mission.)

Mom's eyebrows arched in surprise. "An evil presence?" She smiled a little. "I doubt it's that bad."

6

"Well, someone should definitely look into it," I suggested. And by "someone," of course, I meant me—it would be a great opportunity to prove to the Superhero Federation that I really do have what it takes. "We could go over there right now and bang on the door and demand they let us toss the place—you know, search it, top to bottom!"

Mom's smile stretched wider. "I think we'll hold off on that for the moment. For now, I think I'll just stop using their products."

I'd had a feeling she was going to say that. But I thought this sounded perfect for me—it had superhero written all over it. I picked up another photo of Howie that was taken just after the near miss with the lighting canister and glanced over my shoulder; poking out from beneath the pink ruffle of my comforter was a corner of the training manual. The manual I'd been ignoring for the last seven days. If I didn't get my almost super butt in gear and start studying, I might never become a full-fledged hero, and I wouldn't be able to investigate this or any other situation. It wouldn't do just to go running blindly toward trouble. Even without studying, I knew that being truly super included being superprepared.

Mom nodded to the laundry basket filled with rumpled clothes. "You'll put those away?"

"Yup." I might have to use nose plugs, but I'd do it. "I'm glad you won't be using this detergent anymore. The smell makes me dizzy."

"Really?" said Mom. "I suppose it does have a stronger scent than other soaps I've used, but it didn't bother me." She reached into the basket, sniffed my yellow sweatshirt, and shrugged. Then she tossed the sweatshirt to me.

I held my breath and caught it.

"And don't just ball it up and stuff it in a drawer . . . fold it!"

I gave her a thumbs-up, still holding the air in my lungs.

"I think I might go and do a little research on that company," Mom said.

I gave a little grunt of agreement, pretty sure I was turning blue.

Looking determined now, Mom marched purposefully out of the room. I waited until the door closed behind her before I tossed the sweatshirt across the room and exhaled gratefully.

Then I removed the manual from where I'd hid it under the comforter.

It was time to get real. Time to be honest with myself. The reason I'd been avoiding the manual was simple: I was scared that even if I studied 24-7, the Superhero Federation would still write me off as a troublemaker who couldn't follow the rules.

And I didn't want to blow it. Something about the way my mom was so concerned about the factory, about the greater good of Sweetbriar, reminded me that being a superhero was just about the biggest deal in the world.

Gritting my teeth with resolve, I opened the manual to page ninety-four.

OVERPOWERING EXTREME VILLAINS
Tips for Beginners

I was going to study like I'd never studied before. For the greater good.

I just hoped it wasn't too late.

CHAPTER 2

I awoke to the sound of whistling coming from the kitchen.

"Come on down, Zoe," Mom called cheerfully. "Breakfast is ready, and I have something to tell you."

I shoved off the blanket and got out of bed, glad that my mom seemed to be in a better mood than she'd been in the night before.

I dressed quickly and bounded downstairs, expecting to find Mom in her pretty yellow bathrobe, sipping her coffee as she admired the garden through the kitchen window. Instead, I found her still dressed in the clothes she'd been wearing the night before, bustling around the table, which was covered with papers—a bunch of computer printouts and several yellow pages torn from a legal pad. From the doorway I could see that she'd scribbled lots of notes—complete with little flow charts, lots of underlined words, and exclamation points here and there. Mom had been *busy.*

9

"I've been up all night!" she announced, not looking even the least bit sleepy. "I was thinking about what you said, you know, about banging on the factory door, and I decided I should do it. Well, not literally, of course. But that factory is hiding something, I can feel it in my bones. So I'm going to take action the best way I know how. "

I smiled. "Let me guess—you're holding a meeting."

In response, Mom picked up the phone and dialed a number.

"Hello, Mary Jane? Maria Richards here. I'm sorry to call so early. . . ."

While she explained to her friend Mary Jane about the factory, Mom pointed to the stove, where a plate was warming on the back burner.

"So you've heard similar rumors, then?" Mom was saying into the phone. "Yes, I'm terribly worried. Which is why I'm holding a meeting at my house this Sunday. That's right, day after tomorrow, at noon."

I cleared an area on the table and sat down with my breakfast: waffles and sausage links. I dug in, glancing at a page my mother must have printed from the Internet.

FEDERAL REGULATIONS
RE: INDUSTRIAL WASTE
Guidelines for Safe Disposal of
Toxic and/or Hazardous Material

Mom had highlighted passages here and there. A hot pink sticky note flagged the corner of the report; she'd written a phone number on it, and I was surprised to find that the number seemed familiar to me. I stared at it, wondering where I'd seen it before. When I heard the beep of the telephone's Off button, I looked up.

"So what's the scoop?" I asked.

"It's still sketchy," Mom admitted. "But I've gotten some solid information from the Internet. And when I telephoned the spokesperson for the factory just a few minutes ago, he was very evasive, even a little hostile. He certainly wasn't about to let me talk to Mr. Mitchell." She paused to eye my breakfast. "How are the waffles, by the way?"

"Delicious," I said, dragging a triangular piece through a puddle of maple syrup on my plate. "But cereal would have been all right, if you were busy. Did you know that Lightning Loops are the official cereal of the Lightning Girl fan club?"

Mom laughed. "Yes, I'm well aware of that. But I'll never be too busy to make your breakfast."

She reached for the phone again and dialed the number that was written on the sticky note. Someone answered and Mom said, "Hello, is this the Devlin residence?"

Devlin? I nearly choked on the waffle. As in *Josh* Devlin? No wonder I recognized the phone number! Back in fourth grade, when I'd first noticed how cute Josh was, I'd gone a little goofy and looked up his digits in the Sweetbriar phone book (which, as any girl who's ever had a crush will tell you, is a perfectly normal thing to do), and just for the heck of it, I'd sort of committed the number to memory—not that I'd had the guts to use it so far.

"Oh, good morning, Josh. This is Mrs. Richards, Zoe's mother."

I couldn't believe it! Josh Devlin was on the other end of that phone line? I couldn't help smiling—until Mom said to Josh:

"Is your mom at home, sweetie?"

11

This time it was a bite of sausage that almost choked me. Did she really just call Josh Devlin *"sweetie"*?

"Sure, honey, I'll hold on."

Honey! I slapped my hand to my forehead in exasperation. "Mom! Couldn't you have called him something cooler? Like . . . dude? Or . . . dog?"

Mom looked at me like I was nuts. "Why would I call Josh a dog? He's a very handsome young man."

I rolled my eyes. "And what are you calling Mrs. Devlin for, anyway?"

"Because," Mom explained, "we've worked together on community service projects before. I thought she might be interested in coming to the meeting."

"I'm going to school now," I announced, getting up from the table and depositing my syrupy plate in the dishwasher.

"So early?"

"I have a big test coming up, and I want to get in extra studying," I told her, which was the truth . . . mostly.

"Well, have a nice day, swee—" Mom caught herself and cleared her throat. "I mean, catch ya later, girlfriend."

Well, at least she was trying. I picked up my school stuff and gave her a grin. "Right back atcha," I said. "And if you need help at the meeting on Sunday, I can pitch in. Maybe we can make some charts or something to show people what information you've found."

"Thanks," she said. "You're super."

I'm working on it, I thought.

I reached Main Street at the height of the morning rush. The sidewalk was busy with people heading to work, carrying huge cardboard cups of expensive coffee.

I marched up to Grandpa just as he was unlocking the front door of Speedy Cleaners.

I got right to the point: "Okay, I don't really get the difference between dodging a proton-charged death ray and deflecting a semiseismic brain melt."

Unfortunately, a woman in a business suit overheard me; she stopped in her tracks, nearly spilling her cappuccino, and stared at me with wide eyes.

I gave her a bright smile. "Science test," I explained.

The woman continued to gape in disbelief.

"She's in the *advanced* class," Grandpa added calmly.

The woman hurried off.

"Nice save," I told Grandpa.

"You wouldn't have needed saving," Grandpa said sternly, "if you'd been a little more careful."

"Sorry."

Grandpa's expression softened into a smile as he held the door open for me.

"I seem to recall that when I was studying for my first super-hero test, I had a little trouble understanding the distinction between brain melts and death rays myself." He chuckled. "You see, it all has to do with the proton projection—and of course, what the bad guy ate for breakfast is always a factor. . . ."

The door to Speedy Cleaners closed behind us, and for all the pedestrians outside knew, it was just another ordinary shop on Main Street.

Grandpa walked toward the back room. I followed him, resisting the urge to hurdle the tall counter.

"First things first," said Grandpa. He flashed a grin at me. "Will you lift the pressing machine for me and move it over there?"

"Sure," I said, easily hoisting the huge metal piece of equipment and carrying it across the room.

I lowered the presser carefully. "Here?"

"Perfect," said Grandpa. He ruffled my hair. "Thank you, Zoe."

He motioned for me to sit as he plugged in the presser and turned on the steam. "Now," he said, "about those death rays . . ."

Fourth period. History.

Ms. Krangle was lecturing about Patrick Henry and some speech he made back around the time of the Revolutionary War.

"Psst."

I turned to my best friend, Emily Huang, who sat in the desk next to me. She was looking straight ahead, but her hand was dangling down beside her chair. She clutched a folded piece of loose-leaf paper between her fingers.

Keeping a casual expression, I gave my pencil a nudge, which sent it rolling across the desktop and over the edge to the floor.

I leaned down to retrieve the pencil, snatched the note from Emily's grasp, and was upright again in a split second (not a superhero skill, just a sixth-grade-note-passing skill). I unfolded the note.

Zoe, come over on Sunday. I've
got two new bottles of nail
polish. We can give each other
manicures and bake macadamia
nut cookies and watch DVDs all
afternoon! ☺

It sounded like fun. But I'd just promised my mother I'd help
her with her meeting on Sunday. I wrote back to Emily:

Sorry! My mom's holding
a meeting at our house
on Sunday and I have to
help out. ☹

I refolded the note and placed it on the corner of my desk.
When Ms. Krangle wasn't looking, I slipped it to Emily under
our desks. She glanced at me and gave a little smile as she
grabbed the note in a lightning-fast motion. Six years of note
passing sure had taught us a thing or two—we were champs.

I watched out of the corner of my eye while Emily unfolded the
note. Her grin faded as soon as she read the first word. She picked

up her pen and wrote something under my reply, but she didn't bother to pass it to me. Instead, she tilted the paper up so I could read the message, which she'd written in large, bold letters:

YOU'RE BUSY—AGAIN?

I guess I couldn't blame her for being disappointed. I'd been making lots of excuses since the superhero thing began. I wrote back quickly:

Please don't be mad. It's a
really important meeting.
The new detergent
factory could be causing
problems to the
environment, and the
whole town—maybe even
the whole planet, the
whole universe—could be
in danger! It would be
socially wimpy of me to
blow it off.

Emily read the note, then giggled quietly. She turned to me
with a smile and mouthed the words

DRAMA QUEEN.

Okay, so maybe the universe wasn't exactly in danger. But still . . .

At the front of the room, Ms. Krangle had plunked a tricorner hat on her head and was standing on a chair, wildly swinging one fist above her head (trust me—if you knew Ms. Krangle, this would not surprise you one bit). She was bellowing dramatically, "Give me liberty, or . . . give . . . me . . ."

Her eyes scanned the room from beneath the brim of her patriotic headwear. When her gaze fell on Howie, she fixed him with a questioning look.

"Um . . ." Howie gulped. "Lunch?"

Ms. Krangle folded her arms across her chest and scowled. "Give me liberty or give me *lunch*?"

"No, ma'am." Howie pointed to the clock above the chalkboard. "I meant it's time for lunch."

Ms. Krangle shoved the hat back from her forehead and eyed the clock. "Ah. So it is." She climbed down from the chair, removed the hat, and smiled at us. "Class dismissed."

CHAPTER 3

I gathered up my books and followed Emily out of the classroom.

"Hey, I'm sorry if I sounded snippy back there," Emily said. "You know . . . that second part of the note."

I shrugged. "It's okay."

We reached my locker. As I worked the combination, Emily leaned against the locker next to mine. "It's just that it seems like we never hang out anymore, ya know?" She gave me a nervous look. "Are you mad at me?"

"No!" I answered quickly. "Of course not." I tugged open the metal door of my locker. "I mean, I miss doing stuff with you. But now that I'm twelve . . ."

. . . my super powers are kicking in and it's up to me to continue my family's heroic legacy as Zachary "Zip" Richards's granddaughter. . . .

". . . my parents expect me to take on more responsibility at home."

Again, mostly true.

Emily sighed. "I know exactly what you mean. My twelfth birthday isn't for two months and my dad already expects me to empty the dishwasher."

I couldn't stop myself from giggling. I was talking about protecting the universe, not washing the dishes, but of course, there was no way to explain that to Emily. I was just glad she understood.

"I have an idea," I said, removing my lunch bag from my locker and swinging the door closed. "Why don't you come over to my house on Sunday? For the meeting."

Emily looked wary. "The meeting, huh?"

As we started down the corridor, I could tell she was remembering the last time she attended one of my mother's activist meetings. It was to raise animal rights awareness, and the cochairperson put Em and me on two straight hours of envelope-stuffing duty. Emily had hated it. I mean, she likes animals as much as the next kid, but even I had to admit that the stuffing job was way boring!

"What's the deal?" she asked. "What's so dangerous about this factory?"

"Mom's heard they're doing stuff that might be bad for the environment," I replied. "Pumping toxic waste or something."

I could see in Emily's eyes that she knew this was a big deal, but before she could comment, someone tapped me on the shoulder.

I turned and came face to face with Josh Devlin. He was so close I could actually see the gold flecks in his green eyes!

"I heard about the factory, too," he said. "I rode my bike out there yesterday to see if I could find out anything, but I couldn't get past the gate."

I was momentarily sidetracked by an image of Josh coasting along on his bicycle with the sun on his face and the wind in his hair. . . .

Emily gave me a little nudge in the ribs. I blinked and made myself pay attention.

"Anyway, my mom's going to your mom's meeting, and I was thinking I might go, too." He glanced away, then back. "That is, unless it would bother you if I . . . ya know . . . tagged along."

I forced myself not to yelp with delight. "Bother me? Why would it bother me?"

"I don't know." He stuffed his hands in his pockets. "I was afraid you might think it was . . . kind of . . . you know . . . weird. For me to come to your house. Not that your house is weird, but . . ."

I knew exactly what he meant: in sixth grade, having a boy come to your house—even for a meeting about toxic waste—could cause big-time gossip. People might think Josh and I were an item or something. I could hear them now: *Ooooooooh! Zoe and Josh sittin' in a tree . . .* and junk like that. So immature! Besides, it wasn't like Josh was coming by to hang out with me; he'd be coming to the meeting because of his concerns about environmental stuff.

Josh's teeth were unbelievably, perfectly, amazingly straight. I heard myself ask, "Do *you* think it would be weird?"

"No, not really." He was looking directly into my eyes now. "Do you?"

It was thoughtful of him to check with me. He knew as well as I did that sixth graders could take something like this and run with it. But if Josh was willing to risk rumors about us being Sweetbriar Middle School's next big couple for the sake of the

22

environment, then so was I. We could be courageous together.

"Nope." I swallowed hard and shook my head. "I think it would be very . . . you know . . . not weird."

Josh smiled.

I smiled.

Emily rolled her eyes.

"Well, I've got to get going," said Josh. "See ya later."

"See ya."

I watched him walk away, all the way down the hall until he turned the corner. Then I looked back at Emily, feeling dazed. "Josh Devlin is coming to my house on Sunday."

"Yeah." Emily quirked her lips into a grin. "I got that."

There was a tumble in my stomach that was part excitement, part panic. "What if it's . . . you know . . . weird?"

"Please!" Emily laughed. "Let's not start that again, okay?"

"Right. Sorry."

We began walking in the direction of her locker. "I guess I won't be at the meeting after all," she said matter-of-factly.

"What do you mean?"

"Well . . ." Emily smiled. "As your best friend, I feel it's my duty to give you some quality alone time with your extremely crushable crush."

I rolled my eyes. "Alone. Right. Just me, Mr. Crush, and a million moms." I laughed, then added honestly, "To tell you the truth, that's plenty alone enough for me!"

"Whatever," said Emily. "It will be great."

We reached her locker; she twirled the lock and pulled at the door once . . . twice. Stuck, as usual.

Absently, I reached in front of her, took hold of the handle and gave a tug. I hadn't meant to use my superstrength, but I guess I accidentally did because the door gave way and crashed open so hard that it dented the locker next to it.

Emily looked at me strangely.

"You must have loosened it up," I fibbed, and quickly shifted the subject back to Sunday's meeting. "So you're sure you don't want to come? We were just saying we never get together any-more. . . ."

"Zoe, chill!" Emily's expression was utterly genuine. "I'm completely cool with it."

I gave her a huge best-friend hug.

"All right," I said. "But next weekend, we're going to do something way best friend–ish. A sleepover, maybe. Or shopping."

"Did somebody say shopping?" Caitlin Abbott was heading toward us, looking like she'd just stepped out of a fashion magazine. She was dressed in one of the funkiest outfits I'd ever seen: lime green flared jeans with a rhinestone belt and a zip-front sweater with oversized faux-fur cuffs. For some reason, the cuffs on her sweater made me think of the costume she'd worn in the play. She'd said that the cuffs were way too long and that she'd used these giant scissors to fix them, but it turned out that she'd lied about shortening the sleeves herself. Something about that had always made me feel a little funny. What had she really been doing with those scissors? But I was in such a good mood I decided not to dwell on it.

Caitlin was giving us her prettiest smile. "My aunt is taking me to the new mall in Templeton Heights this Sunday. Anybody wanna come along?" She looked from Emily to me, then back to Emily. "They've got all the best stores and a food court that's so big it almost has its own zip code."

Emily gave me an awkward look.

"This Sunday?" I asked glumly.

Caitlin nodded. "They're having all kinds of grand opening sales."

"Thanks anyway, Caitlin," I said. "I can't make it." I nodded to Emily. "But you should go."

Caitlin turned to me with a sympathetic sigh. "Maybe you can come next time, Zoe."

I was about to say that I'd like that, but she turned back to Emily as though she'd already forgotten what she'd just said. "Walk with me to my locker, and we'll plan our shopping strategy."

"Okay." Emily pulled her lunch pack out of her locker. "Do you mind, Zoe?"

I shook my head. "Not at all. I hear there are forty-seven shoe stores on the first floor alone. You're gonna need all the strategy you can get."

"We'll see you at the lunch tables, then!"

They took off down the hall and I headed the other way, toward the doors that led outside. I couldn't blame Emily for wanting to go to the mall.

But I *could* feel a little left out.

And I *could* feel more than a little nervous, because there was something about Caitlin that made me suspicious.

I could . . . and I did.

But by the time next weekend rolled around, my superhero exam would be behind me (I hoped I'd pass with flying colors), and I'd be spending some quality time with my BFF. Unless, of course, some extreme villain got his death ray up and running, or I got called away to some far-off planet to prevent an alien invasion.

But I wasn't going to dwell on that, either.

CHAPTER 4

On Saturday afternoon, I was in my room studying for the superhero test when Mom called up the stairs.

"Zoe, will you please come down here for a moment?" There was a chuckle in her voice. "You have a visitor."

I tucked the manual into the drawer of my night table and went downstairs.

"Who is it?" I asked, hopping with both feet onto the lowest landing.

"Well," said Mom, making a sweeping gesture with her arm toward the foyer, "I *think* it's your grandfather... but it's difficult to be certain."

Sure enough, a man stood in the middle of the entry hall, holding a big tackle box in one hand and clutching a fishing pole in the other. He was dressed head to toe in outdoor gear— a gray nylon vest with about a zillion pockets on it, a pair of tall, green rubber wading boots, and a floppy canvas hat with fishing lures pinned to its brim, which hung down so low over his face that I couldn't see his eyes or his nose.

I laughed out loud. "Grandpa Zack, is that you under there?"

"SURE IS!"

"What's with the getup?"

Grandpa put down the tackle box and pushed his hat back. "Did you forget about our fishing trip?"

"Um . . . well . . ." I *hadn't* forgotten about our fishing trip because we hadn't *planned* any fishing trip. But he winked at me, and I knew I was expected to play along with the charade. "Yes. I forgot all about it."

"Well, throw on an old pair of jeans and a sweatshirt. I closed the shop early, I've got plenty of bait, and I know a great spot along the Sweetbriar River where the fish practically jump out of the water and into your hands."

"Then what do we need bait for?" I joked.

Mom laughed. "I think it sounds like fun, as long as you're planning to follow the catch-and-release rule. So where is this amazing fishing spot?"

"Oh, it's way out past the town limits," replied Grandpa. "At the end of Shady Bank Road."

"Really?" Mom was suddenly on alert. "Near the detergent factory?"

I shot Grandpa a look.

"NOT <u>TOO</u> NEAR,"

he answered.

27

"Hey, Mom," I said quickly, before she could start making a big deal about the location, "do you think you could fix Grandpa and me a couple of sandwiches for the trip while I go get changed?"

"Good idea," said Grandpa. "I work up an appetite when I go fishing."

After Mom had disappeared into the kitchen to prepare our feast, I whispered to Grandpa, "What's up?"

"Training exercises. And we're going to need lots of room." He gave the zipper on his fishing vest a little tug. "*Lots* of room."

"Oh." That sounded . . . challenging. "So the fishing expedition is just a cover?"

Grandpa nodded, and I could feel the excitement rush through me. This was real secret agent–type stuff. We were establishing a *cover*. Cool.

I hurried up the stairs to change. After a quick search of my closet, I chose a pair of holey blue jeans and a faded old sweatshirt. Then I quickly wound my hair into two loose braids and slapped a frayed ball cap on my head. I sure didn't look like a superhero-in-training; I looked like a kid going fishing with her grandpa. Perfect!

"I'm ready!" I cried, clattering back down the stairs. "Fish, beware!

Mom had returned from the kitchen and was holding a picnic basket. "You'll have to be a lot quieter than that if you expect to catch anything," she advised.

"I'll be quiet," I told her, to keep from blowing my cover. I took the picnic basket and kissed her good-bye. "In fact, I'll be *super*quiet."

28

Grandpa's secret spot had nothing to do with fishing. It was a place on the outskirts of town where the span of the Sweetbriar River was at its widest—nearly fifty feet across from one grassy bank to the other. We stood on the woodsy side; the other bank opened into a broad stretch of grassy meadow that was usually dappled with thousands of purple and pink wildflowers.

"Where are the flowers?" I wondered aloud, frowning across the field at the ugly gray factory in the distance.

"Huh?" Grandpa was busy surveying the width of the river. "What flowers?"

"The ones that used to grow wild in the meadow. Look."

He gave a quick glance over his shoulder, then did a double take. "You're right," he said, shading his eyes from the bright sunshine and scanning the expanse.

There was not a single petal in sight, just dry grass and brown stems with dead leaves and shriveled heads.

It was a depressing scene. I turned away. It seemed that Mom's hunch about the factory was a good one; even without proof, it wasn't much of a jump to imagine that something connected with the factory could be the cause of the dead flowers. I made a mental note to mention it at tomorrow's meeting.

"So why are we here?" I asked. "Is this where I learn to bring the entire river to a boil by shooting laser beams out of my eyes?"

Grandpa shook his head. "Not today."

He opened the tackle box, and I could see that, other than a few faded bobbers and a tangle of old fishing line, there was nothing inside that had anything to do with catching fish.

Grandpa removed what looked to be a cross between a digital camera and a handheld calculator—only a zillion times more intricate, with flashing buttons and switches and something that looked like a miniature satellite dish attached to the corner. He pressed a button on the gadget and it whirred to life.

"What's that?" I asked.

"A measuring device." Grandpa marched along the bank a little way until he found what he was looking for: a dead oak tree had fallen across the river, creating a bridge.

"You'll need to come back from the other side."

"Come back?" I put my hands on my hips. "So I guess that means I'm going across the river."

"Correct."

I stared at the water, taking in the width from bank to bank. The current looked pretty strong, and I could tell just by looking that it was deep. And cold.

"And how, exactly, am I going to get to the other side in the first place?" I asked.

But I had a pretty good idea.

CHAPTER

5

THE day's lesson was going to be all about, as Grandpa called it, "airborne transport via forward propulsion." Also known as jumping.

"I can already jump," I argued.

"I know you can," he said. "You jumped across the stage at the school play."

"So why do I have to practice?"

Grandpa put his hands on my shoulders and looked me in the eye. "Zoe, you know as well as I do that you got lucky with that jump."

I remembered the way I got my leg hooked in the scenery and almost blew the entire rescue. He was right. I got lucky.

"Airborne transport can be very useful to a superhero," he explained. "It's not a power exactly, it's more of a skill. Your speed and strength enable you to jump high and far, but as for aim, accuracy, and control—those things must be learned."

"I'M READY."

"Good girl. All right, then, toes on the bank."

Obediently, I stepped toward the slope of the riverbank and settled the toes of my sneakers on the edge. This sent a tiny avalanche of dirt and pebbles rolling down toward the water. "How's this?"

"Excellent. Now, bend your knees. . . . A little deeper. . . . No, not that deep. . . . Yes, that's right." Grandpa pointed across the water. "Now, I want you to focus on a spot in that meadow, oh, maybe three yards beyond the opposite bank, where the ground is flat and solid. If you land too near the slope, there's always the chance you may lose your footing and slide backward."

I squinted into the brightness of the sun reflected on the water. "Focused."

"From this position, using your heels, you're going to spring up and out. Got that? Up, but not straight up. When I was learning, I made the mistake of going completely vertical and smacked my head on the underside of a helicopter."

"Ouch."

"Indeed."

"Up and out," I repeated.

"Yes. The key words are *forward propulsion.*"

"Wouldn't I go farther if I gave myself a running start?" I asked.

"Maybe. But consider this—you could inadvertently gather too much speed, which would increase the velocity of the jump, thus making it that much harder to control. And besides, rescue scenarios don't always allow for a running start."

"Hadn't thought of that."

"Yes, well, it was a logical question. Now . . . here we go."

I concentrated on the spot across the river.

"Trust that your strength will carry you," Grandpa whispered. "It's in you, Zoe. All you have to do is leap. As soon as your body recognizes that gravity is against you, it will call upon the depth of its own power and take over the jump. Soon you'll be able to decide to use your strength, but for now, you only have to trust your superhero instincts and . . . *jump!*"

I jumped. I kept my eyes forward and launched myself off the earth, springing upward, outward. . . .

I felt the precise nanosecond that the power took over. What began as an ordinary gym-class-caliber track-and-field long jump became a sonic hurdle! It was as if my body just decided to ignore gravity. The jump stretched higher, farther, longer. . . . I was twenty-five feet up, then thirty, with the water rushing below me. I'd never felt anything like it—I was a little bit scared, a lot excited, and totally super! My blood pounded in my veins like a drum solo in a rock 'n' roll song!

"Focus!" Grandpa called from the bank.

But it was at that moment that I noticed the vat.

It was the bright orange lettering on the side that caught my eye. I shifted my gaze from my landing target to the factory. From the wooded side of the river, I had only been able to see the upper stories of the building. Now that I was airborne, the entire factory was in view, and I could see all the way down to ground level, where a huge vat stood beside the foundation wall.

Stenciled on the side of the vat was the word HAZMAT.

"Focus!" Grandpa cried again.

But it was too late. I forgot all about the jumping exercise, and the minute I forgot, my body downshifted from Super mode.

33

"Uh-oh."

You know those cartoons where the coyote accidentally runs off a cliff, and for a few seconds, his legs keep pumping and he just sort of hovers there in midair before he goes plummeting down...down...down...

Well, I was that coyote.

"Ahhhgggg!"

SPLASH!

Grandpa ran across the fallen-tree bridge and met me as I climbed up the bank on the opposite side of the river. My excessive dripping had turned the dirt to mud, which made for a slippery climb.

"What happened?" he asked. "You were off to such a terrific start."

"I know," I said, collapsing in a wet heap in the grass. "But then I noticed something that broke my concentra—"

I gasped as a familiar smell sent my brain spiraling.

"Zoe, what is it?"

"I'm dizzy!"

"Must be from the fall."

"No! It's the smell."

Grandpa sniffed the air.

"Do you smell it?" I demanded.

"Yes! It smells like..." Grandpa gave me a puzzled look. "Like apple blossoms. No, like eucalyptus. Wait... it's more like... a breeze through a field of heather."

"Mountain-fresh-country-ocean-autumn-sunrise...," I sputtered. I closed my eyes tightly, but I could still feel the spinning in my head. "It's the smell that's making me dizzy!"

With every breath I took, floral and citrus and herbal bombs seemed to be exploding all around me. Then it occurred to me that I wasn't just *smelling* springtime-sunshine-wildflower-blah-blah-blah, I was *tasting* it, too. I must have gotten a mouthful of river water.

"Yuck!" I knew it was impolite, but I couldn't help it: I had to spit. When I did, Grandpa looked shocked.

"Zoe, you're spitting bubbles!"

And I was. A sparkly trail of soap bubbles drifted from my lips and floated toward the sky.

I spit until the soapy taste was gone; then I sat still and waited for the wooziness to pass. When I felt better, I explained to Grandpa about the new detergent Mom had used and the dizzying effect it had had on me. I was certain the two episodes had to be connected, and that they were more than likely linked to the factory's waste output.

"Mom's hunch was right," I said, feeling anger churning inside me. "She had a feeling Mr. Hazmat was polluting the river. She's having a meeting about it on Sunday."

"Mr. who?"

"Mr. Hazmat. He must be some dodgy business partner of Mr. Mitchell's, because his name is painted in great big letters on the side of a giant vat." I was proud of my deductive reasoning. "So all we have to do is find this Mr. Hazmat, seeing as Mom couldn't get through to Mr. Mitchell, and tell him what's what."

"Actually . . ." Grandpa cleared his throat, his eyes twinkling. "*Hazmat* is an abbreviation for *Hazardous Material*."

I felt my cheeks flush with embarrassment. "Oh."

Grandpa helped me up; I waited until he had made his way

back across the makeshift bridge. Then I positioned myself on the bank and sprang up and across the river. This time, I cleared the water and landed on the opposite side with no trouble at all.

"Nice one," said Grandpa. "Good steady landing."

"Thanks."

"And as far as this whole waste issue is concerned," he continued, "I'll see what I can find out about it as soon as we get home. In the meantime, we've got more training drills to do."

I was just getting ready to attempt a second jump when we heard my mother's voice calling through the trees.

"What's she doing here?" I asked Grandpa in an urgent whisper.

He shrugged. Mom emerged from the woods, carrying my fishing pole.

"Thought you might need this," she said. "How in the world does a person go fishing and forget to bring along her fishing pole?"

"Good question," I mumbled, then forced a laugh. "Guess I'm not gonna be voted *Field and Stream*'s Sportsgirl of the Year, huh?"

Mom looked me up and down, taking in my sopping wet jeans and dripping sweatshirt. "What happened?"

"Um . . . well, you see . . . I had this big fish on my line . . . this *really* big fish. . . ."

"Huge fish," said Grandpa. "Enormous."

"And I was trying to reel him in. . . ."

Mom quirked an eyebrow. "Without a pole?"

"She was using mine," Grandpa offered quickly.

"Right." I picked up Grandpa's fishing pole from where it leaned against the tackle box to demonstrate. "But I wasn't used to Grandpa's reel, and since the fish was so gigantic, I sort of lost control and got pulled into the river."

"Are you all right?" Mom asked.

"I'm fine. Just a little wet." I handed Grandpa his fishing pole and took the one my mother was holding. "I shouldn't have any trouble now that I've got my own pole."

I fiddled with the reel for a moment. I hoped Mom wasn't going to wait around to watch me bait the hook. We didn't have any bait. We didn't even have any hooks, unless you counted the lures attached to Grandpa's hat.

But Mom wasn't looking at me; her gaze was fixed across the river, beyond the meadow. She was scowling at the factory with a very determined look in her eye.

I knew that look! She was planning something. And it didn't take a mind reader to imagine what it was.

CHAPTER 6

"I think I'll go over to the factory gate and take a closer look," said Mom.

I hadn't meant to yell, but I didn't like the idea of my mother wandering around over there. Sure, I didn't have any solid evidence that Mitchell Enterprises was up to no good... but then, I had no way of knowing that it wasn't, either. And although all I'd found so far was some soapy water, it was certainly possible that this guy was up to something much worse. And if that was true, chances were he wouldn't look kindly on Mom's snooping.

"Don't go!"

"Why not?" asked Mom.

"It's trespassing," said Grandpa.

"Not if I stay outside the fence," Mom argued.

Grandpa nodded reluctantly. "Good point."

I searched for a reason that might change her mind. "I'm interested in this issue, too, and I'd like to join you in looking for clues, but I can't go with you right now because Grandpa and I have more fishing to do."

Mom gave my shoulder a squeeze. "I appreciate your interest, Zoe, but since I'm here, it would be silly not to go over there and check out that factory on my own."

I slid Grandpa a look. I could tell he didn't like the idea of Mom walking into a dangerous situation, either.

"Zoe and I can go along with you on your search," he said to my mother. "We can fish some other time."

I felt a surge of relief. Maybe I wasn't allowed to use my super-powers yet, but I was sure that as a retired hero, Grandpa could protect Mom and me if anything came up.

"Good. Let's go."

As we walked along the riverbank, Mom eyed the dead grass in the field. I could practically see the wheels turning in her head; I'd have bet a million bucks she was thinking the same thing I'd thought—that the factory was responsible. She turned away from the brown meadow and looked at the water.

"I think you gave up on your fishing too early," she teased. "Looks like there's a big school of fish swimming down there." She pointed to a trail of bubbles, then frowned. "That's an awful lot of bubbles."

I grinned. "Maybe it's not just a school. Maybe it's a whole *university* of fish."

But as the bubbles popped, I smelled flowery soap.

"When I was a little girl," my mother said, "back before the Sweetbriar city council built the town pool, the river water was so clean and clear that we used to come here and swim." She sighed over the memory, while I dragged my hand across my lips, which still tasted soapy.

"I wouldn't recommend that now," I said.

"Neither would I!" Mom stopped in her tracks and pointed down the sloping embankment to the water. "Zoe, Zack . . . look."

We looked. The end of a wide metal pipe—a newly installed one, from the shiny look of it—poked from the reeds. Spilling out of the pipe into the beautiful river was a stream of green goop. When the goop hit the water, it made a hissing sound and created a thick film of brownish green foam.

"That can't be good," I said, wrinkling my nose.

"It's not," Mom agreed. "And it's certainly enough reason to launch an official protest. That looks disgusting!"

She was right. This was proof that something was being dumped into the river. In which case, the hazmat vat was just for show, since the waste was being routed right into the Sweetbriar.

"But why would someone dump this stuff in the river? Don't they know how bad that is for the environment?" I demanded. There had to be safer ways of getting rid of this nasty green sludge.

"It can be very expensive to dispose of dangerous chemicals properly," Grandpa explained. "But some people are more concerned with making a quick buck than protecting the ducks."

I couldn't help smiling at Grandpa's rhyming explanation. But as I thought about the ducks, I stopped smiling. They lived in that water. I was in the river for a few measly seconds, and I came up spitting soap bubbles. I could only imagine what was happening to the ducks, fish, frogs, and everything else that lived in the river.

More than ever, I wanted Mom to expose whatever Mr. Mitchell was up to.

And more than ever, I wanted to help.

40

On Sunday morning, I helped Mom prepare for the meeting. We set up an easel in the living room to hold a large map of Sweetbriar. Mom stuck in a red pushpin to indicate the factory's location. Then she used a yellow highlighter to outline the river while I laid out flyers on the dining room table, next to the trays of snacks we'd put out for the guests: lemon squares, shortbread cookies, and coffee cake. I was feeling pretty psyched about the meeting. It was going to be way more intense now that we had evidence!

"I'll finish up," said Mom, replacing the cap on the highlighter with a little snap. "You go on upstairs and get dressed."

She didn't have to tell me twice! Josh Devlin was coming to this meeting and I needed to look great. I dashed upstairs, careful to keep from breaking into superspeed.

In my room, I'd laid out four possible outfits. I studied them now, trying to decide which one was the most activist-ish ensemble. I wished I could call Emily for fashion advice, but I knew she would already be on her way to the mall with Caitlin.

It took me a while, but I finally settled on a pair of gray corduroy pants with a ribbon belt and a pink polo shirt. Then, for extra environmental cuteness, I added my endangered species charm bracelet just as the doorbell rang.

I stepped into the hall and listened eagerly. Sure enough, I could hear my mother inviting Mrs. Devlin and Josh inside.

Smiling like a nutcase, I headed down the stairs. Mrs. Devlin was hanging her jacket on the coatrack; Josh had made his way over to the map.

"Hi, Mrs. Devlin," I said when I reached the bottom landing.

"Hey, Josh." I sounded calm, but I was gripping the banister as tightly as I could without shifting into Super mode. I was still new at this boy-girl thing, but I was pretty sure smashing the railing with my bare hands wouldn't be considered good flirting form.

Two more attendees had arrived just behind the Devlins, and while Mom ushered them inside, I joined Josh at the easel. I picked up the plate of lemon squares Mom and I had baked and held it out to Josh. My bracelet jingled happily.

"Cool bracelet," Josh said. "Is that a bald eagle?"

I held up my wrist so that the light caught the charm and flashed off the round head of the tiny eagle. "Yep. Every charm represents an endangered bird, mammal, or reptile. This one"— I pointed to the smallest trinket—"is a Choctawhatchee beach mouse."

"What's that squirmy-looking one?"

I twisted the bracelet around so I could grasp the charm. "This is a Coachella Valley fringe-toed lizard. It's my favorite. I love its pointy toes. And when I shake my arm, it really does seem to squirm."

"I like it."

He liked it. I made a silent vow never to go anywhere without wearing that bracelet!

Josh smiled and bit into his lemon square just as the phone rang. I excused myself and went into the kitchen to answer it.

"Hello?"

"Zoe? It's Grandpa."

"Hi, Grandpa."

There was a short pause. "I need you to swing by the cleaner's. I have something important to show you."

"Okay, sure." I peeked around the kitchen doorframe and

42

watched Josh helping himself to a cup of punch. "As soon as the meeting is over, I'll—"

"Now, Zoe."

"Now?"

I peeked into the living room again. More of Mom's activist friends and acquaintances had arrived. People were passing the flyers around and sounding interested and excited, and Josh looked so cool in his SAVE THE WHALES T-shirt. Surely whatever Grandpa wanted to show me could wait. Just then, Josh turned in my direction and waved at me. I nearly dropped the phone.

"I'll be there, Grandpa," I said, returning Josh's wave. "Forty-five minutes, tops."

"Zoe, I realize your mother's meeting is about to begin, but—"

I didn't hear the rest of Grandpa's sentence because now Josh was smiling at me.

"So, Grandpa, I'll see you in about an hour?"

"Zoe!" Grandpa's voice was so loud that I had to hold the handset away from my ear. "You must come to the store at once. This can't wait."

"Okay, okay!" I crept farther into the kitchen, pressed the phone to my lips, and spoke in a whisper. "What's so important?"

"A message," said Grandpa, more quietly. "From the Superhero Federation, Department of Punishable Offenses."

It took a moment for the words to sink in.

"Zoe?"

"I'm on my way," I managed to croak.

I hung up the phone, went back into the living room, and approached Josh.

"You're not going to believe this," I said, forcing a chuckle, "but I've got to leave."

"Leave?" He frowned.

"Yeah, but I'll be right back," I said, trying to smile. *I hope I will, anyway,* I thought as I dashed off a note to my mom; the words "Punishable Offenses" were ringing in my ears.

I hurried out the door, hoping for the best...

...but prepared for the absolute worst.

CHAPTER 7

THE little bell on the front door of the cleaner's jangled when I stepped inside. Grandpa nodded to me but didn't smile. I decided to try my luck with Gran.

"How's it goin', Gran?"

"Hello, Zoe dear." Her eyes looked worried. That made me feel worse—Gran knew all about my superhero training, even though she wasn't a Super herself.

"Sally," said Grandpa, "will you watch the counter, please?" He didn't wait for an answer; instead, he crooked his finger at me, then stepped through the curtain that led to the rear of the shop.

I took a deep breath and followed him.

Grandpa's office was a small, boxy room tucked in the back of the dry-cleaning store. There was a desk under the window, where he kept track of his paperwork. On the desk in a brass frame was my fifth-grade school photograph. As Grandpa took his seat behind the desk, I motioned to the picture.

"Worst haircut I ever had," I said, laughing a little. "And look at that sweater! What was I thinking?"

Grandpa said nothing. So much for conversation.

I watched as he opened the top drawer of the desk and removed a plain business envelope addressed to me, care of Speedy Cleaners. It was postmarked and everything, and looked totally official. That sort of threw me; I was expecting a more high-tech form of communication. The only thing out of the ordinary about this envelope was that it had no return address on it.

"It's a letter," I said somewhat stupidly.

"I told you it was a letter."

"You said it was a message."

"A letter is a message."

"Yeah, but I thought it would be something more . . . ya know . . . technological."

He handed me the letter. I just held it for a long moment, stalling, I guess.

"So the Superhero Federation uses the U.S. Postal Service."

"Why not?" Grandpa's tone was even. "It's perfectly reliable."

I opened the envelope and removed a sheet of average-looking cream-colored stationery with the Superhero Federation logo emblazoned at the top.

Dear Superhero in-training,

As you know, the Super Federation expressly forbids apprentice-level superheroes from utilizing their powers prior to completing phase one of their training, which includes taking and passing exam one of the superhero assessment process. We are writing to let you know that we have learned of your recent unsanctioned superhero activity.

Before I could read further, the page in my hand started to tremble. The letters began to shift, moving outward toward the margins, sliding across the surface like a water bug on a pond, leaving the center of the page blank, but only for a split second. I shook my head to clear it, but it wasn't just my eyes going googly with shock. The letters really had scooted to the edge of the page. They were replaced by a graphic that sprouted right up out of the paper, a three-dimensional image like one of those pop-up illustrations in kids' books. But this was no ordinary cardboard foldout. The image was animated, made of light and shadow, like a teeny tiny movie playing in the palm of my hand.

I stared down at the letter, amazed to recognize a miniature version of my school auditorium flickering on the page. It was actual footage taken the day of the final rehearsal for the school play.

I looked at Grandpa, astounded; a smile played around the corners of his mouth, but he kept his voice stern. "High-tech enough for ya?"

The pop-up scene was showing Howie onstage with Emily, and I was there in the wings. Then I was jumping across the page and crashing into the set, just like I remembered it. At that point, the pop-up movie stopped flickering and flattened itself back into the page. The words skidded from the margins back to their proper places, which I figured meant that I should read on.

So I read on:

> **It is with the utmost seriousness that we, the staff of the Department of Punishable Offenses, do hereby notify you that you are being placed on Apprentice Probation, effective immediately. With the exception of officially supervised training sessions, you are not, under any circumstances, to use, display, or otherwise employ your powers. Failure to abide by this warning will result in instantaneous dismissal from the apprentice program.**
>
> **Respectfully yours,**

I had just gotten to the signature at the bottom when the paper began to glow. It went from cream-colored to electric yellow to bright purple. Then the paper shriveled up and disappeared in a puff of smoke.

Okay, so as far as stationery goes, I had to admit, the Superhero Federation had some unbelievably cool letterhead. But that didn't change the fact that the correspondence had contained the worst possible news I could have gotten.

I was on probation.

Last Chance Saloon.

One more strike and I was out.

In other words, I was in trouble.

It felt like a million years passed before Grandpa got up from his chair and joined me on the other side of the desk. The office still smelled of smoke from the disappearing message; it made me remember the way Gran's dining room had smelled right after I'd blown out my twelve (and one for good luck) birthday candles just a few weeks before—the night I found out I had superpowers. That seemed like a *trillion* years ago.

Grandpa put one hand on my shoulder. "I think you're beginning to understand how important this is," he said.

I nodded hard but kept my eyes fixed on the floor.

"The Superhero Federation is a powerful institution, Zoe. The most powerful in the entire galaxy. They do not hand out any sort of punishment without giving the situation careful consideration first."

"Baloney!" I said.

Grandpa looked at me in surprise. "Excuse me?"

"This is just a bunch of baloney!" I said more loudly. The nervous feeling I'd had when I started reading the letter had morphed into anger.

"I *had* to use my powers that day!" I went on. "If I hadn't, Howie and who knows who else would have been hurt. What did the

49

Federation expect me to do? Let my friends get squashed? Yeah, sure, I broke the rule—I used my powers sooner than I was supposed to, but c'mon, I saved someone's life! And these Federation guys are worried about my *timing*? That's just nuts!"

Grandpa was staring at me with his mouth open. I began to stomp around the office.

"It's not only nuts, it's unfair. You can't punish someone for doing something good!" I stopped and planted my hands on my hips. "Maybe I'm not cut out for this whole superhero thing. If the big bosses would rather I let my friend take a light fixture to the skull than use my powers ahead of schedule, then maybe I don't want to work for them."

For a moment, Grandpa didn't seem to know what to say. "This probationary period is for your own protection as much as for the whole galaxy's safety," he said at last.

"What about Howie's safety?" I demanded. "The Federation is a bunch of hippopotamuses!"

"Hypocrites," came Gran's voice from the doorway. "I think you meant to say 'hypocrites.' "

"Yeah. That's what I meant. Hypocrites. They want me to develop instincts and take care of the world, and then when I do, they go and pitch a fit just because the rules say I'm supposed to wait. Well, I bet Howie's glad I didn't wait."

Gran laughed. "Excellent point. I agree with everything you just said. Well, except that part about not working for the Federation." She crossed the room, then braced her hands on my shoulders and looked me directly in the eye.

"You have the mighty blood of Zip in your veins, and because of that you will *not* quit. I simply won't have it. I suggest you make a formal appeal and tell those big bosses, as you call them, that you think the rules need to be tweaked a bit. You have every right to do so. Give them a piece of your mind, girl. Maybe they'll see reason. But in the meantime, you're going to get through this probation, pass that blasted test, and carry on the family legacy . . . *and* you're going to be darn good at it."

I thought for a long moment. "Are you sure you're not just saying this to make me feel better about the whole probation thing?"

"Positive." Gran's eyes twinkled. "When you're right, you're right. And besides, I spent the last two weeks working on *this* little beauty!" With that, she produced what she'd been clutching behind her back. It appeared in a flourish of pink and green—zippers shining, snaps glinting in the fluorescent light of the office.

My supersuit.

<u>MY</u> SUPERSUIT!

As it swayed gently on its hanger, I could only stare at it—a two-piece ensemble that consisted of a shirt and a pair of pants. They were just about the coolest articles of clothing I'd ever seen, and I was pretty sure Emily would agree with me. I could tell Gran was still working on the suit because some of it was held together with straight pins, and several loose threads hung from the seams. But I knew that when it was finished, it was going to be fabulous.

The top was basically just a long-sleeved shirt, designed with broad hot pink and brilliant green stripes. Pinned to the shoulders was a flowing cape of shimmering pink fabric. Gran had marked the hem; it would come down to about the middle of my thighs. On the front of the shirt was my superhero logo. It was just like the symbol Grandpa had shown me the night he revealed the big secret, but this one was embroidered in pink and green to match the suit.

The bottom part of the outfit was just as awesome to behold. The pants were green, with a bunch of cargo pockets and utility loops attached. They were cuffed at the knee, and I could see that Gran had sewn heavy-duty knee pads inside. I had already received a pair of superindestructible pink and green boots to complete the outfit.

"Fashionable and durable," Gran pronounced. "*Very* durable."

Grandpa reached out and touched one of the sleeves. "Dry clean only, of course."

"The cape is fireproof," Gran boasted. "Not to mention ultra-absorbent."

"You made this for me?" I said in a hushed voice. "Even though I haven't even taken my test?"

"Yes," said Gran confidently. "We have absolute faith in you. We know you're going to succeed."

"Here's another little something you might like," Grandpa said, reaching into one of the file cabinet drawers and withdrawing a green knapsack.

"A backpack," I said, though I guessed it was probably a whole lot more than just a backpack.

"This is where you'll store the supersuit when you're not wearing it," Grandpa explained. He gave one of the many zippers a shake. "These are unmeltable."

"Clever."

"The fabric looks like everyday nylon," he explained, "but actually, it's made by the Federation specifically for use by superheroes. It won't snag, rip, shred, or fray."

"Wow."

"I've been trying to talk the Federation into marketing it to pantyhose manufacturers," Gran added. "So far, no dice."

I giggled.

"The pockets each serve a particular purpose." Grandpa indicated each of the outer compartments and rattled off its function. "Digital tracking devices go here; truth serum vials slip securely into these pouches; code-breaking equipment is kept in this compartment, and intergalactic communication tools fit here."

I took the backpack and examined it closely.

"The straps can be detached and used to restrain villains," Grandpa continued. "The entire thing is laser-proof, which means it can double as a shield against any variety of ray-emitting weapon. Oh, and if you tug this flap three times, the backpack will glow in the dark."

"Neat." I took hold of the zipper that secured the front pocket and checked out the three little items that were clipped to it. They looked like key chains, the kind every kid in my class had hanging off his or her backpack. One was a minicheeseburger made out of rubber. The second was a yellow smiley face pom-pom, and the third was a plastic pennant that read COOL KID.

I tried to imagine what I'd be able to do with these gadgets. Probably transmit top-secret information around the globe, or maybe spray memory-erasing gas, or see through brick walls.

"What do these do?" I asked eagerly, jiggling the gadgets through my fingers. "These things that look like regular key chains."

Gran and Grandpa exchanged a look. "Those *are* regular key chains," said Grandpa. "We put them on because we thought you'd like them."

Oh. Well . . . that was good, too. I was crazy about cheese-burgers.

Gran gave me a wink, holding out the suit again. "Try it on."

"Really?"

"I want to check the length on that cape. I think they're wearing them a little shorter these days."

I took the hanger and hurried out of the office into the fitting room where Gran's customers tried on clothes for her to alter. I tore off my own clothes, then removed the supersuit from the hanger.

I got a little tangled in the cape trying to get the shirt over my head, and the pants had so many buttons, hooks, and zippers that I thought I'd never get them fastened.

When I finally got the pants on, I felt something in the front pocket. I reached in and pulled out a figure-eight-shaped scrap of green fabric.

MY <u>MASK</u>.

Reverently, I placed it over my eyes and secured it behind my head with its elasticized strap. Then, drawing a deep breath, I turned slowly toward the full-length mirror and looked at myself. Zoe Richards, superhero.

Well, almost.

A volcano of pride erupted inside my chest as I marveled at my reflection. I seemed to be standing straighter than I ever had before, and there was a bold upward tilt to my chin.

A surge of confidence filled me, despite the mistakes I'd made so far, despite the probation, and despite the fact that I didn't fully agree with some of the Federation's rules and regulations. *I can do this,* I thought. Gran and Grandpa believed in me.

And suddenly, for the first time since discovering that I was

destined to be a force of good and justice in the universe, I believed in myself.

CHAPTER 8

MOM'S meeting was over when I got home. I carried the backpack into the house hidden under a pile of Dad's freshly dry-cleaned shirts that Grandpa had sent home from the shop. Just knowing I had the backpack was making me smile my head off.

Mom looked pretty happy, too.

"I guess the meeting went well," I observed, placing the backpack near the stairs.

"Very well," said Mom, taking the leftover lemon squares into the kitchen. "As soon as I told them about the waste pipe we saw dumping sludge into the river, everyone jumped right on board. We've planned a rally at the factory for Saturday."

I grabbed a few empty plates and cups and joined her at the sink. "That sounds exciting."

"Speaking of exciting . . ." Mom had a little smile on her face as she crossed to the refrigerator. "Josh left this for you." One of the meeting flyers was folded and stuck to the metal face of the fridge with a chrysanthemum-shaped magnet, next to my last geography test, the one with the huge red A+ on it. Mom removed the flyer and handed it to me.

I unfolded the flyer and saw that Josh had written a short note on the back of it. I immediately folded it up again for fear of fainting on the spot.

Oh, man! What an amazing day this was turning out to be. first the supersuit and an indestructible backpack, now this! A note from Josh Devlin in his very own handwriting (which was a little on the sloppy side, but hey, I could live with that)!

"He's a very nice young man," said Mom, but her smile faded. "I wonder if Howie will feel bad about your receiving notes from another boy."

Ugh. I'd forgotten that Mom was under the impression that Howie Hunt was my boyfriend. I'd had to use that fib a couple of times to cover up for superhero stuff. But seriously, how could I ever have Howie as a boyfriend? In first grade, we used to sit in the backyard and have contests to see which of us could stuff the most marshmallows into our mouth.

"C'mon, Mom," I said, rolling my eyes. "It's a puny little note, it's not a dozen long-stemmed roses! And besides, it's not like Howie and me are married or anything!"

"Howie and *I*," Mom corrected automatically. "I'd just feel awful if you broke poor Howie's heart."

I saved poor Howie's life, I reminded myself silently. To Mom, I said, "Don't worry. I won't."

I took the note and left the kitchen, seizing my superbackpack on my way up the stairs. After tucking the backpack into the closet, I sat on the bed and opened the note.

Dear Zoe,

Too bad you had to leave.
The meeting was cool. I'm
jazzed for Saturday. Want
to have lunch together
tomorrow and go over the
plans for the rally? Give me
your answer in homeroom.

Josh

My toes tingled. But it had nothing to do with shifting into superspeed!

"KNOCK, KNOCK."

I looked up from the note to see Emily poking her head in the door.

"Hey, Em!" I cried, jumping up from the bed and pulling her into the room. I'd been missing her even more than I realized. "I'm so glad you came by."

"Me too." Emily was toting four huge shopping bags. "Caitlin's nice and all, but we have very different shopping styles, and, well, she wouldn't split a hot fudge sundae with me at the food court. She wanted to go to the juice bar instead, where they only use organic fruits and they don't add any sugar. It was like drinking fresh-squeezed lawn clippings!" She gave me a puppy-dog look. "I kept wishing you were there."

"Thanks," I said.

She noticed the flyer in my hands. "What's that?"

My cheeks turned pink. "A note," I said. "From Josh."

Emily opened her mouth. She closed it. Her eyes danced. "Shut *up!*"

I grinned. "It is."

Emily snatched the note and belly flopped onto my comforter, facing away from me. Her feet dangled over the side of the bed as she devoured the words. "Gosh, could he be any cuter?" she sighed.

I seriously doubted it.

Emily got right down to business. "Okay, well, I think you definitely should buy hot lunch tomorrow. It's a lot more sophisticated than brown-bagging it." She bit her lower lip thoughtfully. "Unless they're serving meat loaf surprise. Oh, and try to snag the picnic table farthest away from the basketball hoops. That one has the most romantic ambiance."

"Okay," I said. I wasn't sure what ambiance was, but I trusted Emily completely.

She bounded off the bed and went straight for my closet. "Now comes the tough part," she warned. "We need to decide what you're going to wear!"

About twenty-seven outfits later, Emily approved an A-line denim miniskirt with a flouncy embroidered tee she'd just bought herself at the Templeton Heights mall. I tried it on while Emily dove (literally) into the task of finding the right shoes, which left her on her hands and knees crawling around the closet floor.

"I'm thinking flats—the navy ones with the rhinestone buckle...or maybe boots...." There was a pause. "Hey, where'd you get this?" she asked. "It's awesome."

I was so distracted with adjusting my skirt that it took me a minute to realize that she'd scooted out of the closet; she was sitting back on her haunches, holding up the superbackpack.

My first thought was *Please don't let it self-destruct.*

"It was a present from my grandparents."

"Oh." Emily put it down beside my tennis shoes. "Love the color. It goes great with your..."

Emily stopped talking. In fact, she stopped moving.

"This can't be good," I muttered, stepping toward her. "Emily?" I bent down and snapped my fingers in front of her face a few times, but she didn't respond.

She was frozen! But why? How?

My eyes shot to the backpack; I dropped to my knees, grabbed it, and shook it. But all that did was make the key chains jingle.

Frantically, I poked into the pockets and compartments but came up empty. Then I noticed the zipper pull tab. It had looked like ordinary metal before, but now it was blinking like a tiny blue Christmas tree light. I squinted at the tab and saw two words engraved into the metal: *Emergency Pause.*

Great. The backpack had somehow zapped Emily, and it had put her on pause, as if she were a CD player. I guess Grandpa

forgot to mention that handy little feature, so I had no idea how to use the zipper to take Emily off pause.

As it turned out, though, I didn't have to do anything. The next second, the zipper stopped blinking blue and began flickering fuchsia. I took that to mean "Time's up," and dropped the backpack where Emily had left it. Then I scrambled back to my feet just as the zipper pull went dark.

". . . eyes," Emily said. Clearly, she had no clue that she'd been frozen for the last few minutes. "Maybe I'll borrow it sometime," she said.

It took me a minute to catch up. "Huh?"

"The backpack," she explained patiently. "It goes with your eyes. And maybe I'll borrow it."

"Oh, uh . . ."

Luckily, Emily didn't wait for an answer. She crept back into the closet and resumed her search for the perfect shoes as I let out a long sigh of relief, making a mental note to ask Grandpa about the zipper zapper.

"One thing I don't understand," she said, her voice muffled inside the closet again. "If you and Josh were together at the meeting, why the note?"

"HUH?"

"Why didn't he just *ask* you to have lunch?" she asked, tossing a patent leather chunky-heeled Mary Jane out of the closet. "You were both at the meeting, so he could have just *asked* you, face to face, up close and personal. Right?"

"Actually . . ." I swallowed hard. "Actually, I kind of had to leave before the meeting started."

It got very quiet inside the closet.

"Em?"

She didn't poke her head out this time. "I thought you said you had to hang around at the meeting to help." There was a note of accusation in her voice.

"I was going to, but then . . ." I fiddled with the embroidery on my shirt. ". . . something came up."

"Like what?"

"Like . . . something."

Silence.

My forehead was perspiring; I felt like I did when I stood on the high dive at the Sweetbriar pool, deciding whether to jump (not that that would ever be an issue again, after my training session the day before). The point was, I felt like I was on the verge of making a huge decision.

She's my best friend. I should tell her.

But the rules say I have to keep the secret.

But she's hurt. She thinks I'm keeping things from her.

I am keeping things from her.

Man, I hate this!

"I had to go out to get something," I said. "For the meeting. We were running low on supplies."

Emily came out of the closet holding my navy blue shoes, which she placed at the foot of my bed.

"You bailed on Josh? You went away and left him here just because you ran out of snacks?"

"Activists love their snacks," I said lamely.

Emily considered the situation. "Personally, I wouldn't have left this house for anything less than chocolate torte." She gave me a sympathetic look. "So you didn't get to hang with Josh at the meeting, but hey, you've got lunch plans, so it's not a bad trade-off."

"True."

"Zoe," my mom called from downstairs, "Emily's father is here to drive her home."

"Okay," I called back.

Emily looked me up and down. "One final adjustment," she said with a grin. She walked back to my closet and pulled out a pair of brown suede boots that came up to my knees. "Try these." I quickly pulled on the boots, then turned back to the mirror to check the effect. Perfect! "Looks great!" Emily declared. She started out the door, then turned back with a grin. "Oh, and if the school cafeteria runs out of coffee cake tomorrow, do me a favor and choose something else. No abandoning Josh for the sake of dessert!"

I laughed. "Don't worry, I won't. See you tomorrow."

I looked at myself in the full-length mirror and smiled. Something told me if the Federation ever got a good look at my best friend, they'd recruit her in a hot second.

I wasn't sure she'd be any better at saving the universe than I would, but I knew one thing for certain: if Emily had super-powers, the world would definitely be a more fashionable place!

CHAPTER 9

LATER that evening—after I'd called Grandpa and he'd explained that the Fast Freeze Feature was the backpack's way of keeping intruders from getting at the contents (it was a recent update he'd forgotten to mention earlier)—I settled down to quiz myself on the superhero training manual.

Seeing how great I looked all decked out in the supersuit had really motivated me, and I was slammin' through the questions like some kind of genius.

What factors must a superhero consider when determining whether to apprehend a villain in a public place?

a. The number of innocent bystanders in the immediate vicinity

b. The weather conditions at the time of confrontation

c. The distance to a local incarceration facility

d. All of the above.

Well, *duh!* All of the above. The bystander thing and the location of the nearest jail were no-brainers. The weather-conditions consideration was a little trickier, but I was prepared for it. Because I'd studied the manual thoroughly and had reviewed the footnotes in chapter four—and because of a particularly exciting Lightning Girl comic strip I'd read the month before—I knew that some villains had the ability to influence atmospheric conditions. If the prevailing weather was right, they could manipulate wind speed, barometric pressure, and air temperature to their advantage, increasing their chances of escape. Not to mention the fact that several of the nastier villains had the power to spit fire, in which case a superhero would be very fortunate if there was a sudden rainstorm about to blow through.

I tallied up my answers and scored the practice test: 99 percent. Good job, me!

It was weird how Electra Allbright, creator of the totally fab Lightning Girl comic-book series, was so good at coming up with story lines that seemed so uncannily realistic. Since I was sure an Ordinary cartoon illustrator would never have seen the superhero manual, I chalked it up to her having a terrific imagination.

Super studying was thirsty work! I decided to take a quick

break and go downstairs to see if Mom had any punch left over from the meeting.

Halfway down the steps, I stopped. Mom and Dad were in the living room, talking. And it sounded serious.

"I'm sorry, Maria. I just don't like it."

"Brian, it's not as though I've never done this before. And besides . . ."

Mom's voice trailed off as she walked out of the living room and into the kitchen. I heard Dad's footsteps going after her. He was saying something I couldn't make out.

I found myself wishing that invisibility were one of my powers. Then I'd be able to follow them and hear every word. Then again, even if I could turn invisible at will, I wouldn't have been able to do it just then, not when I was *on probation*.

So I had to rely on the one power every kid has: the power of sneakiness!

Hopping from the midpoint step to the landing, then from the landing to the floor, I dashed across the living room area rug and flung myself behind the sofa just as Mom and Dad were coming out of the kitchen. I peeked around the edge of the couch and listened.

"Remember the last time you held a rally?" Dad was saying.

"Of course I do," Mom replied cheerfully. "We were demonstrating at the high school to protest the new school superintendent's book-banning policy."

"And do you remember how it ended up?"

"Hmmm." Mom flopped down on the love seat and pretended to search her memory. "If I recall, it ended with the mayor, the high school principal, and me chained to the school library's circulation desk singing 'America the Beautiful' in three-part harmony."

Dad gave her a mock scowl and sat down next to her.

"Oh . . ." Mom smiled sweetly and snapped her fingers as though she'd just remembered something. "*And* the super-intendent resigned that very afternoon and all of the so-called offensive reading material—*The Adventures of Huckleberry Finn*, for heaven's sake—was returned to the high school library." She beamed proudly.

"Maria, you're not dealing with a high school superintendent here. George Mitchell is a very wealthy man, and in business, that means power. He's not going to sit back and let people cast doubt on the way he runs his factory."

I switched my gaze to Mom, waiting to see what she would say next. She didn't disappoint me.

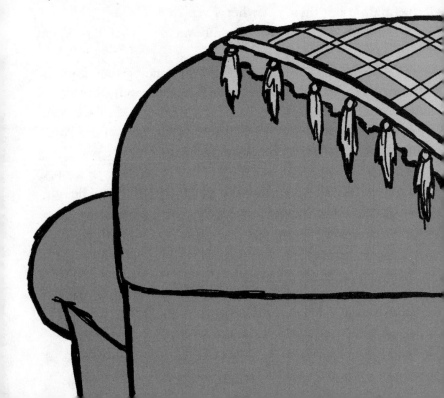

our concern," she said, her face serious now,
at George Mitchell is rich and well connected
license to destroy the environment. I have a
n to publicize what's going on at that factory."

Way to go, Mom! When she talked like this, it was easy to imagine how she'd been a great student activist.

Dad thought for a long moment. Mom and I held our breath.

"I'll tell you what," he said at last. "Since this means so much to you, and since the environmental angle is a significant one, I'll call the chief and volunteer to be at the rally on Saturday. That way, I can keep an eye on you *and* George Mitchell."

Mom squeezed his hand. "Thank you."

Relief washed over me. We were still going to make our protest!

Dad got up and went to his den to make the call. I waited behind the sofa until Mom picked up a home décor magazine from the coffee table and became engrossed in it. As quietly and quickly as I could (without violating my probation), I scooted out from behind the sofa and back to the landing, then took the stairs on tiptoe.

I felt a little nervous. Grandpa and I had suspected that Mitchell was big trouble, and now Dad's remarks confirmed it. There were going to be a lot of concerned citizens at that rally on Saturday. If Mitchell got mad enough, who knew how he'd . . . what was that word Dad had used . . .

RETALIATE.

A shiver went down my spine. I didn't like that word. I didn't like it at all.

CHAPTER 10

FROM the moment I woke up on Monday morning, I couldn't stop thinking about my lunch date with Josh. I managed to wrap myself in Emily's baby blue sweater and spent extra time on my hair. As soon as I got to school, I checked the lunch menu and heaved a sigh of relief. The cafeteria was serving French bread pizza for lunch—*way* sophisticated. Everything was going to be perfect.

The first four class periods crept by like sleepwalking snails, but finally I found myself heading out to the lunch tables, tray in hand, and hoping no one had snagged the romantic table farthest away from the basketball hoops.

No one had, but it looked like a couple of seventh graders were eyeing it; it was all I could do to keep from busting into superspeed to beat them to it. Luckily, the seventh graders decided to eat their lunch under a tree near the soccer field, so I made my way over to the table and took a seat.

I'd just opened my milk carton when I spotted Josh coming out of the lunchroom with his tray.

Shoot! What should I do? Wave? Jump up and shout, *"Josh, over here!"*? Then everyone would know Josh and I were going to have lunch together—which, come to think of it, wasn't the worst that could happen. Or should I just be cool and wait for him to find me? Or . . .

"Hey, Zoe."

I looked up to see Howie Hunt sliding onto the bench across the table.

"Howie! What are you doing?"

"I'm having lunch. What do you think I'm doing?"

Okay, I'll be the first to admit that I don't know a heck of a lot about romance, but I was pretty sure that having Howie Hunt as a third wheel was pretty much the definition of mood kill.

"Are you sure you want to sit here?" I asked a bit desperately. "I mean, wouldn't you rather sit somewhere less . . . romantic?"

He looked at me like I'd grown another head.

By then, Josh had spotted me—correction: *us*—and was on his way over. I wished the superhero manual had included a chapter on how to get rid of extreme Howies, but *no*—all the Superhero Federation seemed to care about was ridding the world of fire-spitting villains. Not that their advice would have made a difference, since I was on probation and all.

Josh arrived and took a moment to size up the situation, looking from me to Howie and back to me again. I felt a little ripple of joy around my heart to see that clearly Josh was as bummed as I was about having Howie in the picture.

He sat down across from me, next to Howie, and I allowed myself to imagine that it was so he could gaze dreamily into my

72

eyes throughout the entire lunch period—and not because the bench I was on tended to wobble when more than one person sat on it.

"So," said Josh, "about this rally . . ." He crunched into his French bread pizza and chewed.

I wished I could take a bite of my own pizza, but I was afraid I'd wind up with a long, drippy string of cheese hanging off my lip. I knew it was kind of a goofy, girly-girl thing to think, but I couldn't help it. This was my first date, after all.

"My dad says the rally is going to require a police presence," I offered. "That's a little scary, isn't it?"

"Scary," Josh agreed, swallowing his mouthful, "but cool. If this Mitchell guy really is polluting our river, I wouldn't mind seeing him handcuffed and hauled away to the hoosegow."

"Hoosegow?"

"It's another word for jail," Howie piped up. "You know, like 'the pokey,' or 'the big house.'"

"Thanks, Howie," I grumbled, shooting him a look that he missed entirely.

Howie opened his backpack and withdrew his lunch bag, which, as always, contained a baloney sandwich, a juice box, and a tangerine. Then he reached into his backpack and pulled out a digital camera. Josh's eyes lit up.

"Like it?" Howie asked, a proud grin on his freckled face. "It's last year's best state-of-the-art model. My uncle got a new one, so he gave this one to me."

"Awesome," said Josh. "I'm into high-tech stuff."

I wondered what Josh would think of my superbackpack. Whatever; it was becoming pretty obvious that I'd done my hair and borrowed Emily's T-shirt for nothing.

"Have a look," said Howie, handing the camera to Josh. "Just be real, real careful."

"This a zoom lens?"

"Yup."

"High-definition?"

"Uh-huh."

"Bet it's got big-time memory capacity."

"Big-time."

I let out an exasperated sigh and took a huge bite of my pizza.

"Hey," Josh said, looking up from the camera and giving me a big smile. "I've got a totally amazing idea."

Since I wasn't about to talk with my mouth full, I just sat there chewing with what I hoped was a "Please tell me because I'm very interested" expression on my face.

"We can go over to the factory grounds," Josh said excitedly, "search for incriminating stuff, and then take pictures of the evidence. That way, when we show up at the rally on Saturday, we'll have visual proof of what the dirtbag factory owner is doing."

Well, that was an amazing idea all right—amazingly risky!

"That is . . . ," said Josh, "if Howie will lend us his camera."

"Oh, no!" Howie slapped both palms on the table. "No way. Absolutely not." He shook his head so hard that his glasses slipped down his nose.

Josh looked disappointed, but I was relieved. What if Josh got caught taking pictures on Mitchell's property?

I gulped down the mouthful of pizza. "Well, so much for that," I said with a shrug. "I mean, without Howie's camera, what's the point in going?"

"Howie can come, too, then."

Both Howie and I stared at Josh.

"What?" I shook my head hard, not even caring if it messed up the hairstyle I'd worked on so diligently that morning.

"It's perfect," Josh continued. "We can go tonight." He looked at me and his eyes seemed to sparkle. "You'll come along, won't you, Zoe?"

Once again, I was distracted by his gaze. Superman had kryptonite; Zoe Richards had Josh Devlin's gorgeous green eyes.

"Well?"

It was obvious from the look on Josh's face that he really wanted to do this. It was also obvious that Howie wasn't going

to let his camera out of his sight, so if Josh went, Howie would be going, too.

Josh looked determined.

Howie looked terrified.

My mind raced through the facts I had so far: Mitchell had something to hide, and from all accounts he was an unsavory sort who'd take drastic action to keep his secret. If he caught anybody on his property—even a couple of sixth-grade boys—he might threaten them . . .

Or worse.

It hit me like a thunderbolt. If anything happened to Josh—or Howie, of course—I would be very, very upset. Especially if it was something I could prevent by going along. I wasn't sure how I'd protect my friends from George Mitchell while I was officially on probation, but at the very least there would be three of us instead of two, and Dad always says there's safety in numbers.

"Okay," I said. "I'll go with you guys."

"Excellent," said Josh, and gave me a high five. It wasn't exactly romantic, but it was better than nothing.

We made plans to meet that evening at six o'clock in front of the school; then we'd bike over to the factory.

Since lunch period was almost over, we gathered up our trays and crossed the yard. Howie was rambling on to Josh about the camera when we passed Emily's table. She was sitting with Caitlin. I tried not to let it bother me, but it did, a little.

"What's with the camera?" Caitlin asked.

"Taking pictures for the yearbook?" said Emily.

"Uh . . . no," said Josh, and caught my eye. He gave me a wink, then went to return his tray to the kitchen. Howie followed him.

"Emily's coming over to my house tonight," Caitlin

announced. "We're going to cut up magazines and make collages to decorate our lockers."

Emily glanced at me, like she was uncomfortable with the way Caitlin seemed to have appointed herself Em's personal social secretary. "Hey, you guys," she said, obviously making an effort to include both Caitlin and me. "I'm going over to the eighth-grade girls' table to ask Megan Talbot where she got that cool eyeshadow. Wanna come with?"

"I've got to go talk to Ms. Krangle about the homework," said Caitlin. She turned on her heel and strode away. I followed Emily toward the eighth-grade girls' table. When she asked about the makeup, Megan gladly informed us that glitter eye-shadow was becoming passé and natural, earthy tones were coming back into style.

On the way to class, Emily kept looking at my eyelids.

"What?" I asked.

"Just wondering if you'd do better with brown shadow or deep violet or maybe..." Suddenly she looked very upset. "Uh-oh."

"What now?"

Emily looked horrified. "Oh, Zoe, I'm so sorry! I didn't notice it before, but... you've got a drippy string of pizza cheese stuck to your chin."

"Do you think it was there while I was having lunch with Josh?" I asked, hoping like crazy that it wasn't.

Emily hesitated. "Probably not."

Great! First Howie ruins my date, and then I find out that I've had pizza cheese hanging off my face for practically the entire lunch period. Not to mention the fact that that night Howie was coming on what could have been my *second* date with Josh Devlin.

I wiped the cheese away, feeling like a total dweeb.

CHAPTER 11

OUR bikes kicked up a small tornado of dust and gravel as we skidded to a halt at the fence that surrounded the factory grounds. The sun had already set, and a gloomy dusk was falling. It was cool and breezy, so I was glad I'd changed into jeans and put on a jacket before I left the house.

We peered through the chain link at the looming building. All the windows were dark.

We parked our bikes and made our way along the fence to the gate. It was chained and locked. Big surprise there. The infuriating thing was that if I had already passed my test, I could have jumped over the fence. Or I'd have been able to use my super-strength to bust the chain and lock with one hand—as long as no one saw me.

"How do we get in?" asked Howie.

"We could try picking the lock," suggested Josh.

"With what?"

We looked around for something sharp to use as a makeshift key, but all we found was a couple of bottle caps, a grungy golf ball, and a Popsicle stick. Nothing sharp, nothing pointy.

I was beginning to squirm with nervousness about what we were trying to do. Squirming like a . . . lizard! A Coachella Valley fringe-toed lizard, to be exact!

"Josh, look!" I thrust my arm at him; the charms of my bracelet plinked and tinkled.

"Excellent!" he said. (He was practically reading my mind! How romantic was that?)

Naturally, Howie was lost. "I don't get it," he said.

I showed him the little silver charm. "Do you know what this is?"

"Sure," said Howie. "It's jewelry. Sterling silver, from the looks of it."

"It's an endangered species charm bracelet, and this charm is a Coachella Valley fringe-toed lizard."

"Pretty scrawny-looking," he observed. "No wonder it's nearly extinct."

I unfastened the clasp and handed the bracelet to Josh. "The point," I said to Howie a bit impatiently, "is that we might be able to use the long, pointy toes to pick the lock on the gate."

Josh was already slithering the silver lizard into the keyhole of the padlock. He bit his lip and looked very intense, and way, way cute.

He jiggled the charm carefully, then twisted. . . .

CLICK.

The lock popped open.

"Josh! You did it!" I was actually pretty surprised that it had worked—I didn't think picking locks was something Josh had a lot of practice with.

"Thanks to you. You were the one who thought of the charm."

"Yeah, but you were the one who figured out how to—"

"Guys . . ." Howie cleared his throat. "Can we do this mutual admiration thing later? It's getting dark."

He was right. Josh handed me back my bracelet, and I clasped it back onto my wrist while he opened the gate just wide enough for us to slip inside.

We ran single file toward the building, stopping when we reached the hazmat container. Up close, it was a lot bigger than it had seemed from a distance. The vat was probably fifteen feet high; it had a metal ladder attached to one side.

"Guys," I whispered. "I think we should check out this vat."

Josh and Howie nodded, and we ducked behind the huge metal container. Actually, Josh and I ducked; Howie tripped and stumbled and clonked his funny bone against the side of the vat. He was about to let out a howl of pain when Josh clapped his hand over his mouth.

"Shhhh! We don't want anyone to hear us."

But Howie's howling would have been the least of our problems. His collision with the metal tank had made a huge noise. The vat was still ringing with a loud, hollow echo.

At that moment, it was one of the most beautiful sounds I'd ever heard. It was the sound of *evidence*.

"This thing is empty!" I whispered excitedly.

Howie rubbed his elbow and pouted. "So? What does that prove?"

"Howie's right!" Josh said, looking troubled. "Maybe the vat was recently emptied, following proper waste-management guidelines. Just because it's empty now doesn't mean it's always been empty."

Good point. I considered it for a moment, picturing the stuff I'd seen pouring into the river, and the foaming water. I just had a hunch that this vat had never been used for its intended purpose. And then I had another thought. I was willing to bet a year's allowance that stuff as gross as that would leave something behind.

"If there had been toxic goop in there," I began, "then even after it was emptied, I'm sure there would still be some . . ." I knit my brows, struggling to remember the word. *Residence? Resume?*

"Residue!" I cried.

"Shhhh!" said Howie.

"Okay," Josh reasoned. "So all we need to do is look inside this vat. If it's got gunky residue clinging to the inner walls, then we know the vat was recently used for holding dangerous stuff. If not, then we know the vat is just here for show."

"Right," I said, thinking of the green stuff Mom and I had seen pouring into the river. "And I bet it will be spotless in there! That's probably the thing that opens the lid," I added, pointing to a big metal wheel near the ladder.

"You guys crank that," Josh directed. "I'll climb the ladder and look inside. Howie, give me the camera."

"No chance!"

"Howie . . ."

Howie clutched the camera to his chest as though it were a favorite teddy bear. "Uh-uh! You'll press the wrong button. Or drop it into the vat."

"No, he won't," I assured Howie.

"It's all right," said Josh. "Howie can climb up and take pictures of the inside of the vat." He glanced at me quickly, then looked away. Even in the dusky gloom I could see that his cheeks were a little red. "Zoe, I'll stay down here with you."

Howie approached the ladder. I happened to know that he'd never been crazy about high places, but if he was willing to overlook that detail, so was I. He tucked the camera in his shirt pocket and started his slow climb.

He took a deep breath and lifted his foot to the first rung; then he cracked his knuckles, rolled his shoulders . . .

Clearly, Howie was terrified. But to his credit, he didn't chicken out. He reached up to grip a higher rung. I actually heard him gulp.

Which, of course, left Josh and me to work the wheel. He took hold of it with one hand; I stood opposite him and grasped it, too.

"Ready?"

He nodded.

"Turn."

We began to spin the wheel; it must not have been oiled, because it took a lot of effort to get it to budge. But when it gave, we could hear the squeak of the lid rising on its giant hinge.

Howie had reached the top of the ladder. Taking hold of the rim of the vat, he stuck his head under the lid.

"Do you see anything?" Josh called in a whisper.

Howie popped his head up. "Nope. Clean as a whistle."

Josh and I exchanged broad smiles.

"That means Mitchell has never used this vat to contain the gunk left over from manufacturing detergent. Which means he must be getting rid of it somewhere else. Like dumping it straight into the Sweetbriar River!"

"We were right!" I gushed. "And the pictures will help us prove it."

"Start taking photos!" Josh called up to Howie. "And use the flash. It's getting darker by the second."

And it was. But I found I didn't mind at all. The sky had turned the color of blueberries, and only a pale pink glow remained on the horizon. The air was cool but not unpleasant, with a mild breeze. I couldn't believe I was standing there, *alone,* with Josh Devlin.

"Good thing you wore your bracelet," he said, "or we'd never have gotten in the gate."

I felt myself blushing. "Good thing you figured out how to use the Coachella Valley fringe-toed lizard charm to pick the lock."

"I guess that means we're a good team."

"I guess it does."

The moment was so amazingly sweet that I began to feel a little dizzy with happiness. A couple of stars had begun to twinkle above, and the whole world smelled of spicy autumn leaves.

And soap . . .

I ignored it. I wanted to just sit there under the stars with Josh and talk about what a terrific team we were. But the breeze carried the scent straight to my nose, and with every windy rustle of the tall grass, the soap smell grew stronger.

Too late, I realized that I wasn't dizzy because Josh was flirting with me, I was dizzy because of that darned soapy smell. And that was when I saw the security guard creeping up to the vat— his dazzlingly clean uniform must have just been washed in the factory's laundry detergent.

"What do you think you're doing up there?" the guard's voice boomed.

Howie was so startled, he bobbled, then wobbled; his foot slipped from the top rung and he began to fall.

Instinct took over and I prepared to execute a superpowered flying leap to save Howie Hunt . . . again! I could feel the power surge in my legs, and I was about to lift off when Josh leaped in front of me from our hiding place beside the vat and positioned himself bravely beneath the swiftly falling Howie. He held out his arms like a fireman prepared to catch a person leaping from a burning building.

WHHHMMPPFFF!

Howie was safe, but it wasn't Josh who'd caught him. It was the security guard, who'd nudged Josh aside in the nick of time and grabbed Howie himself.

"Gotcha!" the guard said, then turned to Josh. "Got you, too."

I was still in Super mode. I knew I could take off into the night and escape. I'd be such a blur of motion that the guard probably wouldn't even notice me. But I couldn't do it. Not just because I was on probation, but because I couldn't bail on my friends.

The tingle of strength fizzed around my calves for a moment more and was gone. I stepped out from the dark shadow of the vat.

"You got me, too," I said.

We waited in the security office for my father to pick us up.

The guard had demanded our phone numbers. He'd called my house first and explained everything to my father, who told him he'd come down and collect the whole lot of us. My mother would call Howie's and Josh's parents to give them the heads-up.

The security office was a small room on the ground floor of the factory, and the smell of the officer's clean uniform was making my stomach turn. I sat on a bench between Howie and Josh while the guard filled out an incident report.

"Where's the camera?" Josh whispered across me to Howie.

"In my pocket," Howie whispered back. "I slipped it in there right after the guard caught me."

"Good thing the guard didn't frisk you."

Howie nodded.

Ten minutes later, the door of the office opened. My father had arrived.

And he *didn't* look happy.

AFTER we dropped off Josh and Howie, Dad headed for our street.

I sat in the backseat, silent. Dad didn't say anything, but I could tell he was fuming. finally he pulled into our driveway and we trooped indoors, still in silence. Mom was waiting in the living room.

I sat down on the sofa, folded my hands in my lap, and waited for the explosion.

"What in the *world* were you thinking, young lady?"

"Do have any idea how *dangerous* that little stunt was?"

"You were trespassing on private property..."

"TRESPASSING!"

"...completely irresponsible..."

"...reckless..."

". . . not to mention *illegal*!"

The words came at me so fast it was hard to tell who was saying what.

Not that it mattered; it all amounted to the same thing:

"You're grounded, Zoe Richards. . . ."

"Do you understand?"

"Grounded!"

Yeah. I understood, all right. "I'm sorry," I said in a tiny voice.

Mom and Dad were quiet for a long moment. I kept my head down while Dad paced back and forth in front of the fireplace and my mother folded her arms and tapped her foot. When they'd had enough of that, they sat down on the couch, one parent on either side of me. When I finally got up the guts to look my mom in the eyes, I realized that she didn't look angry anymore.

She looked . . . guilty.

"I'm sorry, too," she said.

This floored me. Dad looked just as surprised.

"What do you have to be sorry for?" I asked.

"I'm afraid I didn't set a very good example the other day," she admitted. "When we were at the factory and I went walking over by the river . . ."

"You did *what*?" Dad's eyes went wide.

"She snooped," I clarified. "But she didn't trespass, honest. She . . . *we* . . . stayed outside the gate."

That got Dad pacing again.

"Maria, a rally with hundreds of people and police protection is one thing. But wandering around by yourselves—"

"I know it was a foolish thing to do," said Mom. "Zoe, you and Howie and Josh should never even have entertained such an idea. What if something had happened to the three of you way out there? No one would have had the slightest idea you were in trouble."

That was true, and if Howie and Josh had gone without me, then I'd have agreed with my mother completely. But what Mom didn't know was that there were probably not too many situations I couldn't have handled. Probation or not, I knew I wouldn't have let anything bad happen to me or my friends.

"You understand that we're only angry because we love you," Mom was saying.

"You're grounded for the next four days," Dad added. "I will allow you to attend the rally on Saturday because it is such an important issue. But if you ever pull another stunt like this, you'll be grounded indefinitely."

"So basically, I'm on probation," I said. This was getting to be a habit.

"In a manner of speaking," said Dad. He sat down next to me again and gave me stern look. "You know we hate punishing you like this, Zoe, but given what you got up to tonight, I think we're being more than fair."

They were, actually. And even though it sucked, I just hoped that when creepy George Mitchell finally got his punishment, the courts would be a lot harder on him than my parents were on me.

The next night, Mom and Dad went to the movies. It was something we usually did as a family, but since I was grounded, I couldn't join them. Grandpa Zack was positively glad to hear I'd had my social privileges temporarily revoked—since I'd be staying with him and Gran while my parents went out, it would be the perfect opportunity for me to take my super-hero test.

As soon as Mom and Dad turned the corner of Grandpa's street, Grandpa and I hopped into Gran's little blue convertible, backed out of the driveway, and took off in the opposite direction. Gran was staying home because (a) although her security clearance allowed her to know about Super activities, she was not certified to attend test sessions, and (b) I was a bit worried that my parents might call to check in or something.

The superhero test! It was hard to believe I was *finally* taking it!

Grandpa guided the car through the streets of Sweetbriar; to anyone who saw us, we would have looked like any grandfather and granddaughter out for a pleasant evening drive. What no one would ever have guessed was that on the backseat of the convertible was a backpack with its own alarm system, containing a newly hemmed and virtually indestructible superhero suit in preteen size 12 slim and a very cool identity-concealing face mask.

Grandpa hadn't said much about where we were headed.

"Where are we going, anyway?" I asked.

"Not far."

Well, that narrowed it down.

We drove on toward the highway. Grandpa merged into traffic and stayed in the right lane, obeying the speed limit.

We passed a sign that read TEMPLETON HEIGHTS MALL NEXT EXIT. I would have loved to ask Grandpa if we could stop at the mall so I could get some new barrettes to match my supersuit, but since that would be a blatant violation of my grounding, I didn't even bother to suggest it.

Ten minutes later, Grandpa flipped on the turn signal and began veering toward an exit.

"Uh, Gramps, the sign says that exit is closed due to construction."

"Yes, it does." He went right on veering.

"Look. The ramp is blocked. There's a flashing light at the end."

"I see that." He calmly drove on, slowing to a stop only when the shiny chrome grill of the car was an inch from the orange cones that closed off the road. The yellow warning light blinked, throwing us in and out of darkness. Grandpa put the car in park.

"We're here," he announced, getting out of the car.

I got out, too, grabbed my backpack from the backseat, and followed him.

The exit ramp led to a gravel road. As far as I could tell, there wasn't a house or even a gas station for miles. Behind us, the sound of cars whipping along the highway faded away as we crossed the unpaved road toward a giant shadowy mass. After another five minutes of walking, I realized that the shadow was actually a huge rocky hill.

I looked up, up, up the side of it. The peak disappeared into the night clouds.

"Do I have to climb this?" I asked.

"Not today."

Grandpa reached out and placed his hand on a crag jutting out from the side of the stony slope.

I heard the grinding sound of rock scraping against rock, and before my eyes a door-sized chunk of the hill slid sideways, revealing an opening.

I smiled broadly. "Way cool."

"I've always thought so."

Grandpa stepped aside and let me enter first. I hesitated,

expecting the inside to be a gloomy, cavernous place with sta-lactites and stalagmites and creepy shadows.

Not even close!

Inside that doorway, under the mountain, was a huge, brightly lit space that made the gymnasium at Sweetbriar Middle School look pretty bogus in comparison.

"Welcome to the Superhero Federation's Training and Testing Facility," Grandpa announced proudly. "It's one of many, of course. We have facilities like this all over the world. In my opinion, this one is the best."

"Why? Is it impenetrable to all natural forces? Undetectable by radar?"

"Well, yes, actually, it's both of those things. But I like it because it has the cleanest locker rooms."

I followed Grandpa to the center of the enormous space.

"This part of your test measures your physical abilities. Speed, strength, balance . . . the basics."

Grandpa explained the test to me. It was like an obstacle course, except that I couldn't see the obstacles . . . yet. That was due to the fact that in actual hero-versus-villain situations, a hero could never know what to expect and had to think on her feet. The obstacles would just pop up, appearing randomly during the test.

"By magic?" I asked.

"Magic is make-believe," Grandpa scoffed. "We superheroes utilize the scientific properties of teleportation and molecular transport."

"Right." I rolled my eyes. "That was gonna be my second guess."

"The lady heroes' locker room is to the left," he said. "Go and suit up."

Just wearing the supersuit made me feel unstoppable. The bright green fabric seemed to shimmer, and the pink accents were pretty and powerful at the same time. I had sleek pockets and barely-there zippers. It made me feel like I was bringing my family's past into the future. I also had a sleek belt that held all my tools. It wasn't clunky, hanging loose like a carpenter's; rather, it fit snugly around my waist, and each compact, high-tech tool was secured to it in a tidy little pouch. Emily would call it a fabulous accessory, I was sure. I skipped out of the locker room and met Grandpa in the middle of what I was beginning to think of as the Super gym. Grandpa gave me instructions while I gathered my long hair into a ponytail.

"Here's how it works," Grandpa said. "When I say go, you jump up to that ledge there." He pointed to one of the high walls. "Choose a tool from your belt and use it to make your way back to the ground. After that, run three laps around the interior . . . top speed, of course . . . and, applying the information you were given in the superhero manual, fight, fend off, or otherwise eliminate any obstacles that crop up along the way. Got it?"

"Got it."

Grandpa winked at me. I took a deep breath. . . .

"Superhero, on your mark . . . get set . . . *go!*"

I jumped!

I jumped with all my supermight and shot into the air like a rocket. It felt so good to be able to use my power freely—it felt like I was born to do it. Which, of course, I was.

I landed cleanly on the ledge, sorted through the tools on my belt, and decided on a long, sturdy rope with a strong-looking clamp attached to one end. Working quickly, I fixed the clamp to the ledge.

"Good girl!" came Grandpa's encouraging shout from below.

Taking a tight hold of the rope, I lowered myself from the ledge, pushing outward. When I swung back in toward the wall, I let my feet hit first, bending my knees against the impact and pushing out again. I'd seen Lightning Girl do it a thousand times in her comic books, but it was even more fun than I expected. Especially when I super-fied the maneuver by flinging myself outward with superstrength, so that I nearly crossed to the opposite side of the enormous gym. Then, on the way back toward the wall, I let myself spin in midair, like a trapeze artist, only superfast.

When I reached the ground, I gave a tug on the rope; the clamp came down. Unfortunately, so did the ledge. It snapped off a section of the wall and crashed down to the highly polished gym floor, right at my feet. I must have used too much strength!

"That will only cost you a tenth of a point," Grandpa hollered. "Keep going."

I returned the rope to my belt and took off at superspeed.

I circled the gigantic room in a mere fraction of a second—once, twice, three times. I must have been just a pink and green blur!

It was amazing. I could feel the speed sizzling in my veins; sparks—actual fiery *sparks*—crackled and sputtered as they were thrown out from my heels. Sparks! How cool was *that*?

But I didn't get to dwell on my fire-breathing feet too long because I could see that the floor at the far end of the gym had slid open and an enormous blast of water was shooting up from the gap. The next thing I knew, a giant tidal wave came rolling across the gym floor in my direction.

I thought fast, struggling to remember what Gran had said about my cape. She'd said the fabric was "ultraabsorbent!" I'd assumed she'd meant it would get all soggy if I ever broke into a supersweat. But maybe . . .

I whipped off my cape and flung it at the wave. The pink fabric of the cape sucked up the entire wave, as though I were wiping up a grape juice spill with a paper towel. The wave was gone; my sodden cape hit the floor with a wet-sounding splat. "Nicely done!" Grandpa cheered.

I resumed running, silently congratulating myself on my quick thinking. That was when the meteor dropped in.

I heard the whistling shriek of its descent and looked up to see a big hunk of galactic stone falling at an amazing speed. Well, I figured I could catch it . . . but then where would I put it while I finished the test? I sure wouldn't want to be lugging a miniature planet around with me if another tidal wave showed up.

I searched my brain, staring hard at the meteor as it came closer . . . closer . . .

I felt a slight stinging in my eyes. Oh, brother . . . I hoped I wasn't about to start crying—that would be majorly unsuper. I clenched my fists against the frustration. I had no idea what I was going to do about the meteor. And what was up with my eyes?

"Zoe!" Grandpa cried. "You're shooting laser beams out of your eyes!"

"I am?"

I was! Two searing red shafts of light were darting out from my eyeballs, aimed directly at the meteor.

"Uh-oh . . . Grandpa, duck!"

He was way ahead of me—he'd already hit the deck and covered his head with his arms.

I turned my laser-shooting eyes to the meteor and concentrated as hard as I could. It kept zooming closer and closer. I gritted my teeth and stared at the center of the space rock. It worked! The lasers did it.

The explosion came like thunder! It was followed by the sound of billions of tiny meteor pieces scattering across the floor.

I wished I'd had a little warning about the laser-beam-out-of-the-eye thing. That was definitely a surprise. Then I realized that it was all part of the test—superheroes never knew what to expect in an emergency situation; the Federation was trying to find out how I'd handle surprises.

I glanced around at the smoking chunks of meteor. I thought I'd handled the surprises pretty darn well!

Grandpa was back on his feet, looking from me to the meteor rubble with an amused smile as he crossed the gym to give me a hug.

"I didn't know I could do that," I confessed.

"Neither did I," Grandpa said. "Zoe, that was amazing!"

"It was kinda neat, wasn't it?"

"Your powers are far more extensive than I thought they'd be at this stage." He smiled. "In other words, kiddo, you've got it goin' on!"

"Is that good or bad?"

"It's terrific. Of course, I'll have my work cut out for me when it comes to training you to use them all! I'd better brush up on the details. I guess I'll be doing some studying of my own."

"Sorry."

"Don't be!" Grandpa hugged me again. "I'm going to enjoy every minute of teaching you to perfect your skills. And I just know that by the time you reach your sixteenth birthday, you'll be proficient at everything from gravitational negotiation to intergalactic mind control."

"Great," I said. "I feel much better now."

"You've done a superbly admirable job so far. I'd say at this point in the test process, you're looking at a solid A." He placed his hand on my shoulder. Suddenly, his eyes looked sympathetic, and he said, "Now comes the truly difficult, demanding portion of the test. Are you up to it?"

I hoped so. The next part sounded really tough. "Bring it on!" I said, bracing myself.

Grandpa wasn't kidding. I could feel beads of perspiration on my forehead. I'd never experienced such pressure, such tension in my life. I was drained, exhausted! The stress was almost painful.

This part of the test was taking all the supereffort I could muster.

"Easy on the grip," Grandpa advised. "You're going to snap that thing in half."

He was right; I eased up on the number two pencil I was clutching.

"Stuck?" he asked.

"No." I scowled at the sheet of paper on the table before me. "It's just that I hate standardized tests. And these word problems . . ."

"Well, they can be tough." Grandpa grinned. "But I seem to recall finishing my apprentice exam with forty-six minutes to spare."

"Overachiever," I muttered. I read the word problem, made my calculations, and colored in a little circle.

"You can do it, Zoe," Grandpa said.

I looked up and smiled at him. "Actually, I've already done it. That was my last question."

Grandpa checked his watch. "Forty-seven minutes to spare," he said with a wink. While I leaned back in my chair and had a good long stretch, Grandpa took my test paper and slipped it into an envelope.

"Aren't you going to correct it?" I asked.

"The Federation handles that," he said. "The active part of the exam was digitally recorded . . . hidden cameras. I didn't mention it before because I was worried you might get stage fright. Anyway, they'll look over the recording"—he tapped the envelope in his hand—"and score this baby at Super headquarters. You'll get your results in a few days."

Oh, great, more waiting around! Between being grounded and waiting for my test scores, these next few days were going to be the longest of my entire life.

CHAPTER 13

IT was Friday afternoon, last class period—Intro to French. Mademoiselle finkelstein was conjugating verbs, but I just couldn't get into it. I had a lot on my mind.

I'd taken the test on Tuesday, but Grandpa had to mail it to the Superhero Federation to be graded, and who knew what kind of backlog they were dealing with in the test-correcting department? It was a little freaky trying to imagine all the other Super kids around the world studying and taking the first-level test, just like I had. Freaky, but fascinating. I wondered if I'd ever get to meet any of them. Maybe there was a superhero Christmas party. Or a big Superhero Federation company picnic, with pie-eating contests and sack races and stuff. Now, that would be something to see! I'd have to ask Grandpa about it. But for now, I was just aching to find out how I'd done on my first assessment. Had I passed? Had I aced it? Or had I totally crashed and burned and they'd zap it back to me with a big fat F written across the top? The suspense was making me nuts.

Being grounded hadn't helped, either. It didn't make me feel any better to know that Josh and Howie had been given the same punishment I had. Boy, did I miss my freedom.

Not that Emily would have been available to hang out even if I'd been allowed to invite her. She was with Caitlin every single minute, it seemed. Shopping, baking, doing yoga with Caitlin's aunt Nina. Not that I would have wanted to join in on *that*. That woman gave me the creeps. Maybe it had to do with the fact that I was such a hot fudge fan; I just couldn't bring myself to trust a person who actually preferred carob to good old-fashioned chocolate. I knew this because it was all Caitlin could talk about. And it seemed to me that she made a special point of inviting Emily to do stuff when I was around. She'd smile and say in that too sweet, too friendly voice, "Why don't you join us, Zoe?" And then she'd look all embarrassed and say, "Oops, I forgot. You're still grounded."

I was pulled from my miserable thoughts when Mademoiselle finkelstein reminded us that we had a quiz on Monday. Then the bell rang and class was over.

"I don't mind tests," Emily remarked as we gathered up our books. "I just can't stand waiting to find out how I did."

"*Oui,* indeed," I replied, cracking a smile. "I totally agree."

After class I walked with Emily to the athletic fields. She was staying after school to play in an intramural soccer game. I would have liked to stay and play, too, but I was grounded. And besides, after the laser beam episode during my test, I was a little wary about playing competitive sports just yet. I didn't want to accidentally blow up the goalie or something.

"You've had a pretty boring week," Emily said, strapping on her shin guards. "You being grounded is almost like me being grounded—you know what I mean? After all, I have my best times with my best friend. Caitlin keeps inviting me to do stuff, but she gets into these weird moods, you know? She can be completely overbearing one second, and the next she's like totally needy."

So Emily didn't think Caitlin was the coolest thing since cable TV after all! Just hearing that made me feel a little better.

"Caitlin's okay," Emily continued. "I guess we're friends. But not best friends, like you and me."

"You're right," I said, feeling proud to be BFFs with a person as smart and secure as Emily. "Sorry if I've been kind of sulky."

"Oh, please!" Emily waved off the comment and pulled on a soccer jersey over her T-shirt. "Being grounded would make anyone crazy! But we're cool. We're always cool." By then, the intramural teams were lining up on the sidelines. Emily and I said good-bye. I watched for a minute as she jogged over to join her team.

Then I—the grounded superhero—headed home.

CHAPTER 14

ON Saturday, I woke up late. Some non-Super part of me must have still been worn out from the test on Wednesday. When I looked out of my bedroom window, Mom and Dad were already loading the car for the rally. I brushed my teeth and threw on some clothes as fast as I could without going all-out Super and was outside in a matter of minutes. After all, this wasn't just my first chance to go somewhere other than school and home since being grounded (apart from the superhero test, of course). Josh would be at the rally, and there was no way I was going to miss a chance to see him.

"Let's go show that factory owner what we think of him!" I said, hopping into the backseat and buckling my seat belt.

"Remember," said Dad, turning the key in the ignition. "We're going to keep this calm and orderly."

Mom and I exchanged looks and giggled.

"Yes, sir, Detective Richards, sir!"

Dad made a funny face and called us a "couple of wise guys," and we were off to the rally.

I couldn't believe how many people had shown up outside the factory. We had to park quite a distance from the gate, but after a long walk we were in the middle of the action. I wished Emily had come along. She would have gotten a kick out of all the different crazy outfits people were wearing. One guy had dressed up like a giant box of laundry detergent with a skull and crossbones painted on it. Em would have appreciated the drama.

There were people carrying hand-painted signs and banners. Someone was handing out little flags with the Sweetbriar town crest on them. There was a man with a bullhorn reminding everyone that the earth belonged to us all and no one should be allowed to pollute it. . . . The usual protest-type stuff.

I recognized several faces from Mom's meeting. Mrs. Devlin was leading the group in a chant: *"find a solution to end the pollution! This is an order—don't mess with our water! Abide by our wishes, stop killing the fishes!"*

Dad gave Mom a hug for luck before he went to join the uniformed police officers near the front of the crowd. I could see in his eyes that he still had some reservations about it all. I guessed it was hard to be an activist's husband and a police officer at the same time.

"Is it okay if I go find Josh and Howie?" I asked my mother.

"Go ahead," said Mom, handing me a picket sign. "But be careful. Stay where you can see me or Dad at all times. And don't wander off. And if things get rowdy, I want you to go straight to the car and wait for us there."

"Okay."

Before she could issue any more warnings, I plunged into the mass of protesters.

"Hey, Zoe!"

Someone up ahead was waving like crazy.

"Emily? Is that you?" I ducked around a tall guy holding a banner that said EARTH: LOVE IT OR LEAVE IT. Then I squeezed between two women wearing matching Greenpeace T-shirts and shouldered my way toward the gate. My Best Friend Forever was waiting there for me, smiling her head off.

"Surprise!" she cried.

I threw my arms around her. "You're here!" When I finally let go of her, she gave me a badge hand-lettered in bright blue and electric purple. It had sliver glitter glued around the edge. It said *Keep Our River Clean*.

"Pin it on," she said. "Everyone's wearing them."

I glanced around and saw that she was right. "Where'd they come from?" I asked.

"I made them! You know, for the rally. Because it's important to you, and that means it's important to me!"

My mouth dropped open. "Wow. Thanks!"

Emily pointed to the badge she was wearing—pink glitter, orange and yellow lettering. "Like the designs? They're part political statement, part fashion statement."

Suddenly, a roar went up from the crowd. Em and I turned our attention from the badges to the gate, which was slowly opening.

"It's George Mitchell," someone beside me whispered as a tall, gray-haired man walked out. He was wearing a dark suit that somehow managed to look a hundred times more expensive than any of Dad's. He was flanked by two burly guys in (less expensive-looking) dark suits and sunglasses, with their hands clasped behind their backs. My gut told me that when these two were schoolkids, they'd spent an awful lot of time in detention for bullying littler guys on the playground.

Mr. Mitchell held up his hands for silence—I was impressed by this show of strength, given the size of the gold watch on his left wrist—and the crowd quieted.

"Good morning, fellow citizens of Sweetbriar," he said in a confident baritone voice. "It seems that we have something of a misunderstanding here. Ladies and gentlemen, let me assure you that I have done nothing to harm the environment. I operate this factory in strict accordance with all state and federal waste-management regulations."

As Mr. Mitchell rattled off a list of codes and policies, smiling all the while, Howie and Josh joined Em and me.

"Did you bring the photos?" I whispered to Howie.

Howie's face went pale. "Oh, no! I left them in the pocket of my jacket in the basket of my bicycle . . . with the camera! I'd better go back and get it!"

"Don't worry," said Josh. "No thief would bother with a jacket in a kid's bike basket. Besides, there are lots of police officers around. Your camera will be fine."

Howie still looked a little panicked.

Mr. Mitchell's speech was interrupted by the sound of beeping behind him. A large Mitchell Enterprises truck was rumbling toward the gate. Mr. Mitchell stepped to one side and waved it through like he was doing the truck driver a huge favor. The driver leaned out the window to nod to the factory owner. His shirt had the name *Charlie* embroidered above the pocket.

As he drove through the gate, he gave his horn another blast. " 'Scuse me, folks!" he barked. "Outta the way, please."

"Hey, Mitchell," called out one of the protesters. "Why don't you show us what's in that truck, huh?"

"Now, why would you want to see what's in the truck?" Mitchell inquired calmly.

"Maybe you're hauling out toxic chemicals," the protester replied. "Prove to us you're doing it by the rules."

Several of the other protesters began to chant, "Show us! Show us!"

Mitchell turned his frozen smile toward Charlie. There was something about the look in the factory owner's eyes that made my breath catch in my lungs.

He gave the truck driver a nod. "Go ahead, Charlie."

Charlie turned off the ignition, climbed out of the truck, and headed around to the back. Josh, Howie, Emily, and I elbowed our way toward the front of the crowd as the protesters gathered around.

Charlie reached for the handle on the door, twisted it, and slid up the back of the truck to reveal the dark interior.

"What is it?" called someone at the back of the group. "What's in there?"

I stared at the cargo. This was definitely not what I'd expected. Judging from the murmur that rippled through the crowd, it wasn't what anyone else was expecting, either.

"Cardboard," someone replied in a tone of disbelief. "Just a bunch of broken-down shipping boxes."

"Tell the people where you're going, Charlie," Mitchell said.

106

Charlie removed his beat-up cap and spoke loudly. "I'm haulin' this cardboard to the recycling facility," he answered. His tone was flat and automatic, like he was speaking from a script. "We do it every day. Once in the morning, and once right after the factory closes for the day. We at Mitchell Enterprises are very serious about takin' care of the environment."

I frowned. Charlie's little speech sounded very rehearsed to me, and I was sure I wasn't the only one who noticed. My eyes shot to my dad. He was frowning, too. I'd have bet a million bucks he was thinking the same thing I was.

Charlie returned his cap to his head, hurried back to the cab, climbed up behind the wheel, and drove away.

For a long moment, the crowd didn't seem to know what to do. They were there to protest about the environment. But they'd just seen proof positive that Mitchell Enterprises followed at least some recycling guidelines. I could imagine what they were thinking: if the company went through all the bother of disposing of cardboard properly, didn't it seem logical that they'd be just as careful with toxic chemicals?

Mitchell gave the crowd an injured look. "As you can see, we are very conscientious. That vat over there"—he waved over his shoulder to indicate the hazmat container—"stores any toxic materials that the plant generates until such time as they can be transported to a proper disposal facility."

Josh, Howie, and I exchanged meaningful glances. We knew he was lying!

"Is that so?" came a familiar voice.

I turned to see my mom making her way toward Mr. Mitchell. The protesters respectfully stepped aside to allow her to pass.

"My name is Maria Richards, and it just so happens that the

other day I saw a pipe emptying toxic gunk into the river!"

Something flickered across Mitchell's face—fury, maybe. Or fear? But he managed to keep smiling. "I don't know what you're talking about," he said in a patronizing tone.

"In that case," said Mom, her voice tight, "let's all take a little walk over to the riverbank and I can show you what I mean."

Mitchell's jaw flexed, and he seemed to grind out his next words. "fine, Ms. Richards. Lead the way."

"It will be my pleasure!"

The crowd hesitated. They seemed to have lost some of their motivation since seeing the cardboard in the truck. But they followed my mother and Mr. Mitchell through the gates toward the meadow and the river. My dad and the other officers went along.

I could feel myself nearly bursting with pride. "Isn't my mom the coolest?"

"She's awesome," Emily agreed. "She even wore practical shoes! High heels would have kept getting stuck in the grass."

Josh, Emily, and I were falling into step with the protesters when I noticed that Howie was heading in the other direction, toward the parking lot.

"Where are you going?" I asked, darting after him (superspeed firmly set to Off).

"To get my camera from my bike basket. We *know* there hasn't been any waste in that vat for ages. I want to take a picture of the look on Mitchell's face when your mom proves that he's a lying snake."

"Good idea," I said.

Howie took off at a jog, and I hurried to catch up with Emily and Josh. Mitchell was probably about to be exposed as a liar anyway, when Mom showed everyone the pipe. Up ahead, I could see my mother boldly leading the march, and I felt another rush of pride. I might have inherited my superpowers from Dad's side of the family, but I definitely got my guts from her!

There was no pipe.

No foam, no sludge. Nothing.

Just the grassy bank and the sparkle of sunshine on the river. The play of sunlight on the water was so dazzling it looked as if someone had sprinkled handfuls of diamonds across the water's flowing surface.

But the protesters weren't noticing the beauty. They were too busy frowning at the water.

"As you can see," Mitchell said smugly, "there is no waste pipe emptying anything into the river."

A murmur of agreement rippled through the crowd.

"But it was here," Mom insisted. "Just a few days ago. I saw it! And the water was bubbling. I saw it with my own eyes."

I was about to shout out that I'd seen it, too, but I didn't figure anyone would believe me any more than they believed Mom.

Then I saw Howie running toward us.

"The pictures!" said Josh. "Howie can show everyone the pictures he took of the inside of the vat. That will prove that Mitchell's a liar."

Howie was clutching his camera in one hand and waving the photos over his head with the other as he drew nearer. "I've got them!" he cried, running along the bank. "I've got— *Oops!*"

He tripped! He managed to cling to the stack of pictures, but his camera went flying out of his grasp in a long, high arc. Josh dove for it and caught it before it hit the ground. Howie, however, was not so lucky.

The crowd watched in horror as Howie staggered on the narrow edge of the bank, then stumbled and fell. He landed hard and rolled down the slope and into the river—photos and all!

"Howie!" cried Emily.

I felt the familiar Superpowered urge to save him, but Dad's officers were fast on their feet. Within seconds, two of them had hopped into the river and grabbed Howie, who came up sputtering. I watched helplessly as the pictures went floating away on the current. I considered jumping in to retrieve them, but I could see that the water had already caused them to run and bleed to the point of obscurity.

"Josh," I said, "does Howie still have the pictures saved on his camera?"

Josh pressed a few buttons and frowned, watching the camera's tiny preview screen. "It doesn't look like it," he said with a sigh. "He must have deleted them when he had the prints made."

I groaned.

Mitchell pretended to look concerned for Howie as the police officers hauled him up the slope.

As soon as it was clear that Howie was nothing worse than wet, the factory owner turned to my mother with a sly grin on his face. "Satisfied, Ms. Richards?"

"Not at all, Mr. Mitchell," she replied calmly. "I know what I saw. And I'm not giving up until I prove it."

His reply was another snakelike smile. Without another word, he started back toward the gate.

The crowd moved like a herd of sheep, following Mitchell. My mom stood at the river's edge, shaking her head in confusion.

After checking to see that Howie was really all right, my dad came over, took Mom's hand, and gently pulled her away.

"I don't get it," I said to Josh and Em. "There really was a pipe sticking out from the bank and spilling yucky gunk into the river."

"Mitchell probably heard about the rally and had the pipe removed," Josh reasoned. "The guy's got money and power. He could have gotten it done during the night and paid his workers extra to keep their mouths shut. No wonder he didn't argue when your mom suggested we all come over here."

"Well, that's good, isn't it?" said Emily, frowning. "If the pipe has been removed, then he's not polluting the river anymore."

She had a point. But that didn't undo the damage that had already been done. I looked around at the dry grass and dead flowers. Mitchell deserved to be punished. And what guarantee did we have that, after the fuss died down, he wouldn't start dumping waste into the river again?

I trudged with my friends toward the gate.

"Thank you all for coming," Mitchell was saying, as though he'd just thrown himself a birthday party and we were his guests. "Don't forget to look for the fifty-cent coupon for my laundry detergent in tomorrow's newspaper."

He waved as the crowd dispersed, then turned on his heel and went back into his big, stupid factory to savor his dishonest victory.

Mom looked angry and embarrassed at the same time.

Dad came up and put his hand on my shoulder. "Let's get going," he said. I could tell he wanted to get Mom home so she could scream or cry or both.

"Actually, Mr. Richards," said Emily, "I was wondering if maybe Zoe and I could go shopping downtown?"

Dad looked at me. I guess my expression told him that I could use a little fun.

"Go ahead," he said. "But be careful. And don't be late."

Dad turned to Howie, who was dripping wet and shivering. "How about I give you a ride home? We can put your bike in the trunk."

My parents and Howie said good-bye and left. I watched them until they reached the gate . . . where I saw something that surprised me almost as much as the truck full of cardboard.

"Is that Caitlin? What's she doing here?"

Emily turned in the direction of the gate.

"I told her about the rally," she replied.

Caitlin was closer now. She waved.

"I'm gonna get going," said Josh. "My parents told me to be home for lunch. Bye, Emily. See ya later, Zoe."

When he was gone, Emily gave me a knowing smile. "He said 'See ya later'!"

"So?"

"So that means you're practically going steady."

I laughed. "It does not."

"Well, it could. Someday."

By now, Caitlin had reached us.

"Looks like I missed all the excitement," she said. "My aunt's morning yoga class ran late."

"Hey, why don't you come downtown with us?" Emily suggested.

"Sounds good to me," Caitlin replied, smiling right at me.

I smiled back, but I couldn't help wishing it could just be me and Emily. Well, maybe this was exactly what I needed— maybe hanging out with Caitlin outside of school would help us to bond. Maybe after this, we'd be really good friends.

Yeah, right. And maybe George Mitchell was one of the good guys.

Caitlin and Emily scooted from storefront to storefront, oohing and aahing over artful displays of scarf belts and cashmere sweaters. There was a raggedy jean jacket-vest that practically made Emily drool. I thought it was pretty cool myself.

"I absolutely *have* to try on that vest," Emily announced. "Let's go in."

Caitlin was already opening the door of the boutique. I had the weird sense that if I attempted to enter, she'd just as soon slam that door closed on my foot as hold it open for me.

"You two go ahead," I said, trying to sound casual. "I'm going to pop over to the dry-cleaning store for a sec and say hi to my grandpa."

"Oh, that's so cute," said Caitlin, her words dripping with insincerity. "You're such a sweet granddaughter."

"Okay," said Emily. "We'll catch up with you there."

I crossed the street and walked the half block to Grandpa's store. I wanted to see if my test results had come. When I entered the dry-cleaning store, the first thing I noticed was the serious look on my grandfather's face. Gran stood beside him behind the counter, looking equally somber.

"Something wrong?"

Grandpa held out an envelope. I recognized the stationery. It was from the Superhero Federation. Uh-oh.

"Bad news?" I gulped. "Again?"

"See for yourself," Grandpa advised. "But I think we should go into the back room."

It didn't take a genius to figure out what had happened. From the way they were behaving, I could see that the letter told us I'd failed. I'd blown it. My throat went tight and I could feel my chin quivering. I followed them into the office, took out the letter and read.

Dear Zoe,

It is with great pleasure

Great pleasure? That sure didn't sound like a notification of failure! Maybe, just maybe . . .

I held my breath and read on eagerly.

that we, the Superhero Federation,

do hereby inform you that you

have been promoted to Superhero, First

Grade, and are, as of this date, considered

on Active Superhero Duty!

My head snapped up from the page and I saw Gran and Grandpa smiling.

"I passed?"

Gran beamed at me. "With flying colors!"

When she said that, three-dimensional streaks of colored light shot out of the page and began to soar around the room like a fast-moving rainbow.

"What are those?"

"Flying colors!" Grandpa said, reaching out to touch a streak of brilliant purple as it shrieked past his head.

I raised my hand and let the pink streak zoom through my fingers.

"Congratulations!" cried Grandpa.

"You guys knew all along!" I scolded, smiling my head off. "That was sneaky!"

For a few minutes, we watched the colors bolt around the room. It was more beautiful than a fireworks display—the colors crossed paths and shimmered, or collided and exploded into smaller streaks of new colors. All for me!

Me. The superhero! Officially on active duty, no less!

Finally, the light show dissolved and the letter did the self-destructing trick I remembered from before. And it happened just in the nick of time—as the light show ended and the letter puffed into nothingness, the front door of the shop opened, its little bell jangling happily as if it, too, wanted to congratulate me.

"Good afternoon, all!" said Electra Allbright, stepping into the store, carrying a pile of rumpled clothes.

"Ellie," said Gran stiffly. "Back in town already?"

"Yes, as a matter of fact." She turned to Grandpa Zack and gave him a glowing smile. "Nice to see *you* again, Zachary."

Electra Allbright, my favorite comic-book writer on this or any other planet, was standing there right in front of me, for the second time in my life. She'd popped into the dry cleaner's just a few weeks earlier when she was in town for a meet-and-greet at Cosmic Connie's Comic Shop. Weird—that was when I'd first discovered that I had superpowers. And here she was now, on the very day that I was being notified that I'd passed my test.

What was even weirder was that Gran knew her well enough to call her Ellie.

"Hi, Ms. Allbright," I said. "Remember me?"

"Of course I remember you, Zelda."

"Uh . . . Zoe."

"Of course. Zoe." She turned back to Gran and dropped her basket of clothing on the counter with a sigh. "I've just returned from a national tour of speaking engagements."

"How nice for you," snapped Gran, sounding as though she didn't think there was anything nice about it. She'd gone from stiff to snippy, and frankly, I couldn't believe it. My grandmother was the very personification of good manners and kindness. I'd never heard her be snippy to anyone!

Electra gushed on. "Oh, I love being on the road. But it's such a whirlwind—personal appearances at comic-book conventions, lecturing at art schools, visiting bookstores. And all those fancy receptions they throw for me certainly take their toll on my wardrobe. Consequently, I've got lots and lots of clothing that needs to be freshened up and pressed."

"You could have had that done 'on the road,' " said Gran.

That seemed like a strange thing for Gran to say. I didn't know much about the dry-cleaning business, but I was pretty sure it was counterproductive to encourage customers to take their clothes elsewhere.

"Of course I could have," said Electra in a sugary voice. "But the last time I was here, you did such a wonderful job. Better than any dry cleaners I've ever patronized.

"I just loved the way Zachary pressed my pantsuits. He's got such a wonderful touch with steam ironing. He flattened my cuffs to perfection."

I was shocked to see Grandpa blush a little. And for a minute, it looked like Gran wanted to flatten more than Electra's cuffs. If I hadn't known better, I would have thought Gran was acting *jealous*. But that was just plain ridiculous.

"So here's the big news," Electra continued. "I've decided to live right here in Sweetbriar! After all, I grew up not far from here, as you know."

I didn't know. Nobody knew anything about Electra Allbright. Correction: Gran and Grandpa knew, apparently. But Electra's personal history was as famously secret as that of her character Lightning Girl. So *how* did they know? And why the heck hadn't they ever mentioned it to me?

"You've bought a house in Sweetbriar?" Grandpa just about choked on the words.

"Why, yes. Nothing too ostentatious, you understand." Electra turned to me. "You know the old mansion up on Sweetbriar Mountain? I sign the papers tomorrow and it's all mine."

"Wow," I said, truly impressed. "That place is awesome."

"Well, it needs a little work," Electra admitted. "I plan to restore it to its former grandeur, the way it used to be in the old days." She batted her eyes at Grandpa. "You remember, don't you, Zack?"

"Let me get this straight," said Gran coolly. "You like the way my husband presses your pantsuits, so you're buying a mansion in Sweetbriar?"

Electra thought for a moment, then pursed her lips in a tight smile and nodded. "Mmm–hmmm. Pretty much."

Gran's eyes narrowed to slits. "Lovely."

She didn't sound as though she found it lovely in the least. I, on the other hand, could hardly imagine anything cooler. The creator of Lightning Girl was practically going to be my neighbor. Oh, man, did I wish I could tell her about my powers! I wished I could let her in on the fact that superheroes like LG didn't just exist in comics and that I just happened to be one. Maybe she'd want to hear all about my heroic adventures (once

I'd had some, that is) so she could use them in her comic books.

Too bad I had to keep my mouth shut.

I watched as Gran put all of Electra's gorgeous clothes into a nylon bag and printed out the slip indicating the day and time for pickup. After Electra had crooned "Ta-ta!" to all of us and made her exit, Gran tossed the bag over her shoulder. It landed on top of a high pile of other nylon bags.

"I've got something for you, Zoe," she said.

She went into the back and returned with a dark garment bag, zipped up securely. Since cleaned clothing was generally returned to customers in clear plastic bags, I had a pretty good hunch what was inside.

I gasped. "My suit?"

"I put the finishing touches on it this morning," said Gran, handing me the bag. "It's ready to be worn. All you have to do is put it in the backpack until you need it."

"When will that be?" I asked in an excited breath.

Grandpa shrugged. "Could be any time."

The bell on the door jangled and Emily bounded into the store.

"Hey," I said. "Where's Caitlin?"

"Still shopping. Her aunt must give her a huge allowance. When I left, she was up to five tops, three pairs of jeans, and a beaded purse." Emily shook her head. "Even I have to admit that's extreme." She shrugged. "Let's go to your house and watch music videos."

"Okay." I kissed my grandparents good-bye, and Emily and I left.

"What's in the bag?" she asked as we rounded the corner of Main Street.

"A suit," I said honestly. "A *business* suit." Also true, since I'd be

120

wearing the suit to do my superhero job. I was pretty sure Emily would assume it was one of my father's work suits. We headed up the hill toward home.

Hugging the garment bag to me, I glanced over the roofs of the quaint downtown district and over the rolling hills toward Sweetbriar Mountain. There, sitting majestically atop it, was Electra Allbright's newly purchased home. It was huge—a little run-down, as she had said, but she was going to fix it up. As Em and I skipped along, I tried to imagine how it would look.

And then I tried to imagine myself, in my supersuit, soaring through the sky above that mansion, with the setting sun glinting in my hair...

...which was why I didn't see the iron lamppost ahead of me.

I skipped right into it!

CLONGK!

"Zoe, are you all right?" Emily cried in a panic.

I couldn't blame her—I'd just crashed headfirst into a big old metal pole!

"I'm fine," I said. There was a pretty good dent in the lamppost, though. Luckily, Emily didn't notice it; she was just relieved that I wasn't unconscious. So was I. I suppose all the superpowers in the world can't save a kid from being an out-and-out klutz every now and then.

Strangely, I was glad about that. It was nice to know I was still at least a little bit normal, even if I was a whole lot super!

CHAPTER 15

EMILY and I made popcorn and watched about six million music videos before she had to go home for dinner.

When she was gone, I finished the popcorn and watched about thirty-eight more videos, everything from hip-hop to heavy metal. Evidently, Mom was still really upset about her rally bombing, because normally she would have told me to change the channel somewhere around the third video. (Mom was not a fan of music videos.)

I brought the empty popcorn bowl into the kitchen and found her seated at the table, going over the original notes she'd made about the factory. She was so intent on her task that she didn't even notice me standing there.

I sat down across from her and waited. The front page of the newspaper was on the table; there was a small blurb about the planned protest rally, but the big news was that the Slink, the diamond thief who'd been plaguing Sweetbriar for weeks, had struck again the night before.

I read the article absently until Mom noticed I was there. When she looked up at me, she seemed defeated, which was not something I was used to. My mom was not the sort to give up.

"You did see it, didn't you, Zoe?" she asked. "You saw the pipe."

"I saw it."

"So it *was* there?"

"It was definitely there."

"I didn't imagine it? The sludge, the foam . . ."

"Nope. You didn't imagine it," I said, thinking of the awful soapy taste I'd had in my mouth after I'd landed in the river.

Frustrated, Mom ran her hands through her hair. "So what happened to it? Where did it go?"

I shrugged. "Mitchell must have had it removed somehow."

"I'm going to get to the bottom of this!" Mom promised.

She bent back over her notes. I decided I might as well get a jump on my homework for the week, so I went upstairs to my room and turned on my computer.

I was greeted with an instant message from Josh.

Justjoshin96: hey
LtngGrlFan: hey
Justjoshin96: waz^
LtngGrlFan: n2m...u??
Justjoshin96: well...
LtngGrlFan: wat???
Justjoshin96: im goin to the factory
now...to c if we missed n e thing 2day

123

```
LtngGrlFan: i dont think thats a good idea
LtngGrlFan: u mite get hurt!!!!
LtngGrlFan: dont go!!!
LtngGrlFan: JOSH!?!?!?!?!!
Justjoshin96: sorry zoe...g2g...cya
LtngGrlFan: JOSH!?!?!?!?!?!
Automated response from Justjoshin96: b
bck soon...got sum thing 2 take care of
```

I flopped back in my chair and dragged my hand through my hair. I couldn't let him go there alone! Who knew what Mitchell might do to a kid like Josh if he caught him snooping around? And what about those two bodybuilding, sunglasses-wearing henchmen of his? I was pretty certain he didn't keep them around for their stimulating conversation. Mitchell had deliberately lied about how he disposed of his hazardous waste. Who knew how far he'd go to keep his secret? I got up from the computer, closed the door of my room, and wrote a note to my parents:

Mom and Dad,

Went to Emily's to

borrow history notes.

Might be awhile. Back

before bedtime.

Zoe

I didn't think my folks would check on me, but I figured they'd freak if they did and found my room empty. Of course, they'd freak even worse if they found the note and believed I was out walking after dark alone, but I didn't have a lot of options at the moment.

I opened the closet and grabbed my superbackpack with my supersuit safely tucked inside. I would have liked to put it on in the privacy of my bedroom, but I couldn't risk running into Josh dressed like a superhero. I could find a place to change at the factory if necessary.

Two seconds later, I was standing on the windowsill with my backpack on my shoulder, looking out over the dusky yard.

"You're superpowered, Zoe," I whispered to myself. "This would only be a dangerous and unbelievably stupid thing to do if you were just a regular kid."

Confident of my powers, I sprang off the sill—the superjump took me across the lawn, over the fence that separated my backyard from Howie's, and onto the sidewalk of Brandon Street. From Brandon it was a straight shot to Route 17, which would take me directly to the factory.

"Here goes nothin'." I took off at top speed. Luckily, no one was out walking on Brandon Street or I'd have been busted big-time!

Boy, did it feel good to run. I'd been struggling so long and hard to keep from using my powers that the sheer relief of letting them take over was amazing. I was born to run like that. My spirit soared as my legs churned. And my mind seemed to be working just as quickly. With every mile I covered, my thoughts about the factory became clearer. All the random hunches and feelings I'd been having seemed to come together into the shape of something logical. By the time I reached the corner of Brandon and Route 17 (in roughly the blink of an eye), I'd come up with a solid theory about George Mitchell and that oh-so-convenient truckload of cardboard.

CHAPTER 16

THE theory made perfect sense, I decided, skidding around the corner and kicking up chunks of asphalt. My feet were buzzing, and my hair was whipping out behind me so wildly it made me wish I'd thought to stick a brush in my backpack.

Route 17 was a woodsy, winding access road that led out of town. Nobody used it much, so I didn't think I'd have to worry about getting caught being super . . . until I saw Josh.

He was way up ahead of me, riding his bike. I could see the red reflectors on his pedals flashing as he pumped them.

If I kept running, I'd blow past him, and even though I was pretty sure he wouldn't be able to tell it was me, I couldn't risk letting him find out there was someone or something bolting around Sweetbriar at warp speed.

I was going too fast to stop short, so I did the next best thing. Still running, I let my knees go soft, then sprang off the pavement like an Olympic hurdler. The jump was amazing—I rose at least fifty feet in the air and covered a distance of a hundred yards. If Josh sensed anything in the sky above him, he probably thought it was a bird. Or a plane. Hey, that sounded kind of familiar. . . .

I touched down on the dark street, taking a few scrambling steps to come to a complete stop. Then I turned and waited for Josh to catch up. It was only a few seconds before he reached me.

"Hey, Josh!"

He hit his brakes and came screeching to a stop, then looked over his shoulder. "Zoe, is that you?"

"Yep, it's me."

I noticed that he was looking at me a little strangely. Then I realized that my hair must have looked like a crazy, wild explosion. I reached up to smooth it.

"New hairstyle, huh?"

"Um . . ."

He smiled. "Looks great!"

"Oh." I felt my superpowered knees turn to ice cream. "Thanks."

"So . . . what are you doing here?"

"Well, uh . . . well, see . . . I was coming to meet you at the factory. But, um, one of the tires on my bike blew out, so I had to leave it." I motioned over his shoulder into the distance. "Didn't you see it back there on the side of the road?" Before he could answer, I barreled on. "I guess you were going too fast to notice it. Anyway, I was going to walk the rest of the way, but now that you're here, maybe you can give me a ride on the handlebars?"

Josh frowned, thinking. I knew as well as he did that riding with someone on your handlebars was stupid and dangerous. What he didn't know was that his passenger was pretty much indestructible. I would never have suggested it otherwise.

"Okay," he said at last. "But only because it would be more dangerous to leave you out here stranded on Route Seventeen in the dark by yourself."

"Right."

I hooked my backpack onto the back of his bike (I was grateful that he didn't ask what was in it; I guess he was too worried about the whole handlebar-riding thing), then settled myself as best I could on the handlebars.

As we rode to the factory, I knew my hair was blowing into Josh's face and I could feel his breath puffing in my ear as he pedaled, and I couldn't help sighing. After all, if my bike really *had* blown a tire, and Josh *had* come along to rescue me, it would have been very romantic, in a fairy-tale sort of way.

When we reached the factory, I sprang off the handlebars and hurried to the gate while Josh was busy parking his bike out of sight. I took hold of the padlock, closed my hand around it, and with only the slightest effort, crushed it into a fistful of metal rubble.

"Look at this!" I said, quickly brushing the metallic powder from my hands. "No lock."

"Lucky for us," said Josh, joining me at the gate. He handed me my backpack and we slipped inside, keeping to the shadows of trees as we made our way across the grounds toward the factory.

"Listen," I said as we walked. "I have a theory. About Mitchell and everything."

"Yeah?" Josh slid me an interested glance. "What is it?"

"That truck we saw today—it was a decoy! I think Mitchell must have arranged for a truck full of recyclable cardboard to just happen to drive by."

Josh considered the idea. "Now that you mention it, that

Charlie guy seemed a little freaked out. And the stuff he said about the factory being environmentally conscious sounded pretty stiff."

"Like someone told him what to say," I said, glad that Josh saw the logic of my theory. "Right?"

"Exactly like that," he agreed. "It sure made Mitchell look good in front of the protesters."

"Yep. And now that Mitchell has had to remove the waste pipe, he's got to have a different way to get the waste to the river. You know, like a plan B."

"I was thinking that, too," said Josh. "That's what I was coming here to find." He gave me a shrug. "But that was as far as I got. I didn't know what I was looking for, I just sort of hoped I'd know it when I saw it."

That was one of the things I liked about Josh. He wasn't afraid to admit he was stumped. Most of the boys in our grade went around pretending they knew everything!

"Well, I think we should start by checking out the trucks," I suggested. "Now that the people in town think the trucks are used to transport cardboard, Mitchell has a good cover. He can load them up with toxic junk and people won't even bother to question him."

"You're probably right!" Josh stopped walking and turned to give me a huge smile. "You're really smart, Zoe."

Ice cream knees again. I grinned. "Thank you."

We hurried toward the factory, which was completely dark. Not a glimmer of light in the whole building. Even though I knew the factory was closed for the night, it still felt kind of creepy.

"C'mon," said Josh. "Let's check the loading dock."

He led me around back, and when we reached the place

where the company trucks and vans pulled up to be loaded and unloaded, we both gasped.

This part of the factory was lit up like a football stadium! And even though it was after hours, the loading dock was definitely open for business. five men were hustling back and forth, shouting instructions to one another. But they weren't wearing Mitchell Enterprises work shirts like Charlie had been; these men were decked out in rubbery-looking hooded jumpsuits, gloves, and protective goggles. The whole scene was really creepy.

I motioned for Josh to follow me. Keeping to the shadows of the building, we crept closer to the dock.

"Back that truck up to the dock, Gus," shouted one of the jumpsuits. "Nice 'n' close."

The one called Gus hopped into the cab and guided the truck backward toward the opening of the loading dock, where three other rubber-clad workers were waiting beside a row of four huge barrels.

"A little more to the left, Gus . . ."

"Cut your wheel, cut your wheel!"

"Brake! Brake!"

The truck slammed to a halt with a grinding squeal.

"Jeesh, Gus. You almost ran over Morty!"

"Sorry."

"Get a move on, fellas. We gotta haul this stuff to the river and dump it before daylight or Mitchell will have our hides."

"Try it again, Gus. Easy does it. . . ."

While the men focused their attention on Gus, Josh and I climbed the four wide steps to the dock, then quickly concealed ourselves behind another barrel.

"Check this out!" Josh whispered.

131

I looked at the barrel. A hideous skull and crossbones stared back at me with hollow eyes and a wicked frown. I didn't have to be a superhero to know what that meant: *poison*.

"That explains the jumpsuits," Josh said. "But what do we do now?"

My first instinct was to charge into the middle of it all and give Gus and Morty and those other finks a supercharged pounding. But I couldn't do that in front of Josh.

"We go back to the gate, find a pay phone, and call my dad," I said reasonably.

"Good idea," said Josh. "Now all we have to do is get out of here without these goons spotting us."

"Right." I leaned out from behind the barrel and scanned the area. "Well, if Goony Gus ever manages to back the truck in straight, we can bolt while they're loading the barrels."

"So I guess we just sit and wait," Josh sighed.

I was about to agree with him when something across the parking lot from the loading dock caught my eye.

And I knew there'd be no sitting and waiting for me.

CHAPTER 17

THE factory was built to form a giant U around the loading dock, so I could see one wing of the building clearly from where Josh and I were hiding. Every one of the windows was dark.

But something had flickered in the biggest window overlooking the dock. A tiny green pin-dot of light had gone on, and its slender beam bounced around the room in a quick sweep before going dark again.

I held my breath. The light flared again, emitting a soft greenish glow.

Someone was in that office! And it looked like they were using some sort of high-tech night-vision light source, which pretty much guaranteed that it wasn't just the janitor coming in to empty the wastepaper basket. Someone was up to no good. Whether it had anything to do with the toxic waste, though, was anybody's guess. I had to find out.

"Josh," I whispered. "I'll be right back."

"WHAT?"

"Shhhh!"

He lowered his voice to a frantic whisper. "We just decided we had to wait until the men were busy loading the truck. You can't go out there."

"I know. But I think I can sneak by them. I'm smaller than you, after all. I want to check out the schedules in the loading dock office. Maybe I can get proof of this after-hours shipment, in case my dad doesn't get here in time."

"I guess that's a good idea," he muttered. "But Zoe, be careful."

I liked that he was worried about me. I gave him a glowing smile. "I will be," I promised. "Now, whatever you do, just keep your eyes on those guys with the barrels, okay?"

"Why?"

"In case they start heading this way to get this barrel. Then you'll have to move fast and go hide behind those cardboard boxes over there."

It was only partly true. They had their hands full with the four barrels they'd already lined up, and probably wouldn't be getting to this one for quite some time. What I really wanted to do was keep Josh from watching me make a superpowered mad dash.

"Good point," said Josh, turning to focus on the guys waiting in the bay.

When I was sure he wasn't looking at me, I scooted out from behind the barrel, and, clutching my backpack, I ran at superspeed directly through the lot toward the opposite wing of the factory.

I wasn't worried about any of the goons spotting me. I was

134

moving at something close to light speed, so I was a mere blur. They would think I was a gust of wind.

When I was close enough, I jumped, shooting upward past all the dark windows and landing on the tarpaper roof of the factory, directly above the room where I'd seen the suspicious light.

I opened my backpack and suited up, finishing with my extremely cool identity-concealing mask. Then I lay flat on my belly and leaned over the side of the building to look in the window.

The room was hazy with green light, but I could make out the surprisingly delicate figure of the intruder. The trespasser was dressed in a black jumpsuit with a hood and face mask and seemed to be searching the room for something specific, going through desk and file-cabinet drawers in a calm, methodical manner. Suddenly, I knew exactly who it was . . . the Slink!

I could have shattered the window glass with a touch of my fingertip, but I thought the sound might alert the guys in the cargo bay. Instead, I reached for my belt and, keeping my eyes fixed on the graceful prowler in the office, felt around until I found my seventy-eight-in-one utility gadget.

I suffered a few frustrating moments of trial and error, locating the hand grenade disengager, the universal jet airplane ignition key, and the nail clippers before I finally found the glass-cutting tool.

Soundlessly, I used it to cut a Zoe-sized hole in the window, gently pulled the glass cutout back and laid it on the floor so it wouldn't shatter, then deftly slipped through the opening. I crouched on the broad windowsill and watched as the trespasser opened a wall safe as easily as if it were a cookie jar.

"Looking for something?" I demanded.

The thief whirled to face me. For a moment I couldn't say anything. That catsuit clung tighter than any standard Lycra, and the person inside it was very definitely *female*!

"Obviously," I said, recovering, "this is George Mitchell's private office, and obviously, that is George Mitchell's private safe." I hopped down from the sill and strode toward the thief. "And obviously, you are *not* George Mitchell."

A wicked little laugh bubbled up from the prowler's throat, followed by a voice that was raspy but surprisingly high-pitched. "And obviously, you have no idea who you're dealing with!"

"I think I do," I said. "You're that diamond thief who's been terrorizing Sweetbriar. The Slinky, is it?" I rolled my eyes behind my mask. "What kind of criminal is named after a toy?"

"It's the Slink, you fool!"

"Whatever." I struck my best hero pose and recited the words I'd memorized from the superhero manual. "By the authority of the Superhero Federation, keepers of justice in the universe, I hereby apprehend you."

The Slink laughed again. "You? Apprehend me?"

With that, she reached into the safe, withdrew a blue velvet pouch, and started to tuck it into a pocket in the snug black jumpsuit.

I lunged for the pouch and took hold of it. "You're not going to get away with this!"

"That's what you think!" The Slink held fast to the pouch and tugged.

I tugged harder.

Maybe a little too hard. The next thing I knew, the pouch tore and the Slink tumbled backward . . . straight through the hole I'd cut in the window!

The contents of the torn pouch—diamonds, hundreds of them!—flew all over the room, but I couldn't collect them then. I sprang back to the windowsill and stuck my head out the window. The Slink had landed safely and was creeping— okay, *slinking*—from shadow to shadow toward the high fence. You had to know she was there to spot her, if you get what I mean. Certainly none of Mitchell's goons noticed there was an intruder in the compound.

I thought fast. Judging from the state of the office floor, it looked as if the Slink had left empty-handed this time, but there was no way I could miss the opportunity to catch her *and* Mitchell getting up to no good. The Slink had robbed pretty much every jewelry store in town! As a superhero, it was my duty to stop her. I scrambled onto the windowsill and jumped down to the ground in the cargo bay.

Admittedly, I didn't land with the same catlike stealth the Slink had, but the goons were too busy rolling barrels into the truck to notice. I knew I had to move fast, before they got to the fifth bar- rel and discovered Josh. I held my breath for a few moments to make sure I hadn't been spotted, then set off after the Slink, using half superspeed so she didn't vanish into a total blur.

Unfortunately, I was so busy tracking the Slink's progress— and trying not to admire the way she leaped onto a Dumpster, then onto the roof of a low building, then actually *ran* along the top of the fence like she was in a highwire act—that I forgot to check where I was putting my feet.

CLANG!

Who left that wrench on the ground? My foot caught the

edge of it and spun it into the air. To save myself from face-planting at warp speed, I managed to go straight into a somersault and land on my feet again. By the time I straightened up, I could only watch helplessly as the wrench sailed through the air and hit the ground, bouncing—loudly—a couple of times. Definitely *not* super.

Out of the corner of my eye, I saw the Slink pause on the fence. She turned to give me a wave—and I just *know* she was thinking something like *I told you you'd never be able to catch me!*—before leaping gracefully to the ground on the other side and disappearing into the shadows.

But failing to catch the Slink was the least of my problems just then.

"What was that?"

Yikes! One of Mitchell's goons had heard the wrench.

"C'mon, let's go check it out," I heard another one say.

"Watch out for that barrel, Morty!" said the first goon.

There was the sound of running feet; then there was a thud, followed by an "oof!", followed by a sinister-sounding crash. I peered around the corner of the Dumpster. On the far side of the loading area, Josh was peeking around the side of his barrel—I just had to hope Gran's fashion-conscious neon pink and green suit didn't catch his eye.

The guy named Morty had knocked over a barrel, sending the lid flying. The shiny green cylinder lay on its side in the middle of the loading zone, and greenish goo was oozing over the concrete. The workers stood in a row with their mouths open, looking utterly horrified. I probably looked the same—the pavement was actually *sizzling* as the poisonous stuff made contact.

"That stuff's deadly! Let's get out of here!" Morty spun around and took off as if he was running for his life. He seemed to know exactly what was in those barrels, so I believed him.

The other goons fled in separate directions. The one closest to the barrels swerved around the last barrel left standing—and collided with Josh. "Look out!" I screamed, but it was too late. The guy didn't even break stride but kept running until he had vanished around the side of the complex. Josh lost his balance and toppled backward, hitting his head on the cement floor with a thud that made me feel sick. I willed him to get up until I was in danger of shooting him with laser beams from my eyes, but he didn't move.

Panic shot through me. The toxic waste was oozing straight

toward him. If it sizzled on pavement, I didn't want to think what it might do when it made contact with a kid!

In one superfast stride, I made it to the loading dock. The poison was only inches away from Josh now, but it wasn't a problem.

All I had to do was scoop him up and carry him to safety. He felt like he weighed less than a bag of sugar. I had just cradled his head in the crook of my arm when I saw his eyes flutter.

Okay, maybe it *was* a problem.

He blinked, then opened his eyes slightly. He seemed to be in a fog. Still, if he saw me . . .

Not good. Not good at all.

His eyes fluttered closed again.

I quickly slid my arm out from beneath his head. Even if he didn't recognize me in my supersuit, I didn't want him to know he'd been rescued by a Super. We superheroes were supposed to remain secret at all times! If Josh opened his eyes and found himself being rescued by a kid in a cape and an eye mask, the world's hugest secret would be blown big-time.

I scanned the area for something I could use to stop the flow of poisonous chemicals. MITCHELL ENTERPRISES in bold red letters caught my eye.

The truck!

I leaped from the loading dock and took hold of the truck's rear bumper. With a grunt, I hoisted the truck off the ground, spun on my heel, and carefully lowered it on its side between Josh and the oozing goop. The metal walls of the truck's bay became an instant dam.

The next second, the toxic spill reached the truck . . .

. . . and the end of its slimy journey.

It pooled, still hissing and sputtering. On the other side of the big rig, Josh was safe.

I bolted to the loading dock office and quickly changed out of my supersuit. Then, since I was there, I gathered up the incriminating schedules and tucked them into my backpack. I was about to jump back up to Mitchell's office to retrieve the diamonds, but I heard Josh calling my name.

I left the office and joined him on the loading dock.

"What happened?" he asked, rubbing his head and sounding groggy.

"Don't you remember?"

"I remember a lady with a knife. That was weird. And then the toxic glop was spilling all over the place and then . . . that's it."

"You must have hit your head pretty hard," I said, feeling genuinely anxious. "Let's go to the office and call my dad. He'll send an ambulance."

I helped Josh up and steadied him as we headed toward the office.

"Zoe?"

"Yes?"

"How'd that truck get up on the loading dock?"

"Umm . . ." I flashed a grin at him. "I guess Gus turned out to be an even worse driver than we thought."

CHAPTER

18

AFTER that, everything seemed to happen in a blur—even to me, the fastest sixth grader in the world.

First, I used the Fast Freeze Feature on my backpack to temporarily stun Josh. I hated to do it, but I didn't have much of a choice. I was wearing my regular clothes by then, but I couldn't let him see me clear everything up before the cops arrived. I set him in one of the office chairs and got to work.

I called the police and left an anonymous tip for Detective Richards about foul play at the factory and five creepy guys in rubber suits who were probably still within the Sweetbriar town limits. I knew if the police traced the call, they'd see that it came from the factory, and figured they'd assume it was just one of Mitchell's employees who'd had a fit of conscience and decided to report his coworkers.

Then I lifted the truck from the loading dock (by now the toxic ooze had hardened into a thick, smelly mass that wasn't going anywhere fast) and returned it to the parking lot because my dad would never believe that it had gotten up there by accident. Josh wouldn't have bought that story, either, I was sure, if his head hadn't been spinning.

Then I carried Josh at superspeed to the gate where we'd left his bike. I propped him on the handlebars and pedaled us both back home (I thought I might have broken the sound barrier halfway down Brandon Street, but I wasn't sure). He came to just as I slowed down in his driveway. He was more confused than ever.

"You passed out again," I said. "I couldn't call anyone because the office at the loading dock was locked. So I rode you home on your bike." I helped him climb down from the handlebars and gave him a serious look. "You should probably have your folks take you to the emergency room, just to be safe."

Josh nodded, then winced at the pain in his head. "I'll just tell them I fell off my bike and hit my head," he decided aloud. "I'm gonna get in a stack of trouble for not wearing my helmet, but if they knew I was at the factory, they'd freak." He looked very uncomfortable, and I knew it had nothing to do with the pounding in his head. "I've never lied to my parents before," he said. "I don't think I'm gonna do it again."

Another thing I liked about Josh: he was honest to the core.

"We learned a pretty good lesson tonight," I said. "In the future, we should leave the crime busting to the professionals."

And by "professionals," of course, I meant me.

I waited until Josh was safe inside his house, then bolted home.

Just as I was sneaking back in through my bedroom window (relieved to find that neither Dad nor Mom had checked on me while I was gone), I heard the phone ring. Two minutes later,

Dad was zooming out of the house, and I knew it was because of the "anonymous" tip.

I put my superbackpack in the closet and yawned as I changed into my pj's. Nothing like a good night's work to make a kid— even a super kid—tired.

I climbed into bed and instantly fell asleep.

The next morning, I went down to breakfast to find my father on the phone providing the details of his long night to his boss, the chief.

"We managed to track down all the employees the tip had mentioned," Dad was saying.

The goons, I thought, suppressing a giggle.

"A guy named Morty ratted Mitchell out on everything." Then Dad mentioned the diamonds that had been found in Mitchell's office. I had almost forgotten about them, but suddenly I was interested. What would a guy like Mitchell be doing with diamonds?

"Mitchell was planning to use them in a new manufacturing process that required something as hard as diamonds to cut metal. Judging by the clues we found at the scene, it looks as if the Slink was trying to steal them but got sidetracked by the commotion in the cargo bay and left without taking anything."

It wasn't a bad theory. I wished I could tell him what had really happened, but of course, I couldn't.

"Two different crimes at one location, Chief!" Dad was saying into the phone. "This is one for the record books."

You can say that again, I thought, stuffing a bite of pancake into my mouth.

Later that morning, I called Josh and asked him how he was feeling.

"The doctor in the ER said it was a pretty major bump, but I don't have a concussion or anything." He paused.

"What?"

"I'm grounded for a week for riding my bike without my helmet, but I feel so bad about lying to them that I kind of don't care about the grounding. Isn't that crazy?"

"No, I don't think it is. I totally understand," I replied.

As I hung up, I actually felt a little envious. Josh had said he would never lie to his parents again, and I was sure that was a promise he would keep. I, on the other hand, had plenty of sneaky excuses ahead of me. All for a good cause . . . but still. I wished it could be different.

I was hanging up the phone when the doorbell rang.

I opened the front door to find Grandpa Zack on the porch. He looked very, very pleased, and he was holding something behind his back.

"Nice work last night, Zoe."

"Just doin' my job," I said, trying to sound modest. "The Slink's still on the loose, though."

"Zoe, you can't get all the bad guys your first time out!" Grandpa stepped inside and looked around. "Are your folks here?" he asked in a whisper.

"No. Dad went down to the police station, and Mom's at the library." I stopped, frowning. "Hang on. How do you know what happened last night?"

Grandpa winked and led the way into the living room. From

behind his back, he produced a copy of the *Supernews*. I read the headline:

KID ZOOM PROVES HERSELF A TRUE HERO

"Who's Kid Zoom?" I said.

"You are!"

"I am?"

"The Superhero Federation gets to choose the names." Grandpa shrugged. "It was between that and Little Zipster."

"EWW!"

"Yeah. I told them you'd say that. So they went with Kid Zoom."

"I like it!"

"Me too." Grandpa took my face in his hands and gave me a kiss right in the middle of my forehead. "Do you have any idea what a great achievement this is? Most heroes don't get a write-up in the newsletter until they've been on active duty for several months. But you, kiddo—*you* make the front page your first time out."

I could feel myself beaming as I read the article at super-speed.

"Can I keep this?" I asked. "I'd like to start a scrapbook like yours so someday I can show it to my Super grandkids."

Grandpa gave me a warm smile. "And you'll be as proud of them as I am of you, I'm sure."

He sat down on the sofa and put his feet on the coffee table. I sat down beside him and put my feet up, too.

"So," I said, folding my arms behind my head, "what's next on the superhero agenda?"

"I don't know." Grandpa folded *his* arms behind *his* head. "But don't worry, we'll find out."

Too right, we would.

And when we did, Kid Zoom would be ready!

ZOE QUINN lives in Maryland with her family and still loves reading comic books. The Caped Sixth Grader books are her first novels.